☆

"Miaow, squeak, purr, yum!"
Mini Moo

☆

"¡Hasta el año que viene, Daisy!"

Angelo

☆

"Spin me faster! Spin me faster!
Spin me faster!"
Daisy

"Eat me! Eat me! Eat Me!"
Stick of candyfloss

☆

More Daisy adventures!

DAISY AND THE TROUBLE WITH LIFE

DAISY AND THE TROUBLE WITH ZOOS

DAISY AND THE TROUBLE WITH GIANTS

DAISY AND THE TROUBLE WITH KITTENS

DAISY AND THE TROUBLE WITH CHRISTMAS

DAISY AND THE TROUBLE WITH MAGGOTS

DAISY AND THE TROUBLE WITH COCONUTS

DAISY AND THE TROUBLE WITH BURGLARS

DAISY AND THE TROUBLE WITH SPORTS DAY

DAISY AND THE TROUBLE WITH PIGGYBANKS

A SUMMER
DOUBLE
DAISY

RED FOX

UK | USA | Canada | Ireland | Australia
India | New Zealand | South Africa

Red Fox is part of the Penguin Random House group of companies
whose addresses can be found at global.penguinrandomhouse.com.

www.penguin.co.uk
www.puffin.co.uk
www.ladybird.co.uk

Penguin
Random House
UK

DAISY AND THE TROUBLE WITH KITTENS first published in 2009
DAISY AND THE TROUBLE WITH COCONUTS first published in 2012
This edition published 2016

001

Text copyright © Kes Gray, 2009, 2012, 2016
Cover illustration copyright © Nick Sharratt, 2016
Inside illustrations copyright © Garry Parsons, 2009, 2012, 2016
Character concept copyright © Kes Gray and Nick Sharratt, 2009, 2012, 2016

The moral right of the author and illustrator has been asserted.

Set in ITC New Baskerville

Printed in Great Britain by Clays Ltd, St Ives plc

A CIP catalogue record for this book is available from the British Library.

ISBN: 978--1-782-95531-3

All correspondence to:
Puffin Books
Penguin Random House Children's
80 Strand, London WC2R 0RL

A SUMMER
DOUBLE
DAISY

Daisy and the Trouble with Kittens and
Daisy and the Trouble with Coconuts

BY KES GRAY

RED FOX

To Minnow.
We miss you.

DAISY

and the TROUBLE with
KITTENS

by Kes Gray

RED FOX

Chapter 1

The **trouble with *gatitos*** is they are sooooooooo cute!!!!

"*Gatitos*" is Spanish for kittens! The waiter I met on our holiday told me.

If *gatitos* looked like slugs instead of kittens, then what happened on our Spanish holiday would never ever have happened. No way José.

If *gatitos* had slimy skin and gungy

bits, instead of cute little whiskers and cute little eyes and cute little noses and cute little paws and cute little everything elses, then I definitely wouldn't have got into trouble on holiday.

I wouldn't have stroked them or given them names or anything.

Or given them bits of my Spanish ham.

How was I to know there would be kittens in our hotel in Spain? Especially kittens that wanted another mum? There weren't any kittens in the holiday magazine that my mum showed me before we went. There were just pictures of our hotel and a swimming pool and a beach. There wasn't one kitten in any of the pictures anywhere.

If you ask me, if hotels have kittens as well as swimming pools, then they should say so in their magazines. But they don't. At least our hotel didn't.

WHICH ISN'T MY FAULT!

Chapter 2

Me and my mum hardly ever go on holiday. We would like to but the trouble is, going on holiday costs ever such a lot of money. Even when it's foreign money, it still costs a lot.

The **trouble with things that cost a lot of money** is you have to save up for them.

If you're trying to save up a lot, it can take ages! You need a huge piggy bank if you're saving up for something as big as a holiday.

Luckily something really really good happened. My nanny and grampy had some money they didn't want, so they gave it to my mum instead!

Mum was really pleased when Nanny and Grampy came round to our house to tell her. She was so pleased she burst out smiling, and then gave them about ten really big kisses!

Then she gave me a big kiss too, and said, "Daisy! Pack your bags – we're going on a summer holiday!"

The **trouble with big kisses** is they can be a bit too big sometimes. The big kiss Mum gave me nearly squashed my nose off!

Once I'd made sure my nose was still on, I ran straight upstairs to my bedroom to pack my bags like Mum asked.

The **trouble with packing your bags** is I've only got a school bag. Actually it's a rucksack, but it's still not that big.

By the time I'd got my toys and my football in it, I didn't have any room left for holiday clothes!

Then my mum came into my bedroom and said, "Daisy, I didn't mean pack your bags right now."

She meant, *Daisy, start thinking about what you would like to take on holiday*, because she hadn't actually booked the hotel yet, and we didn't actually know where we would be going yet, and we wouldn't actually be going anywhere for about a month!

Then my nanny and grampy came into my bedroom and said it would probably be better if I left my football at home and bought a blow-up beach ball instead. That would give me much more room in my rucksack.

Then they gave ME some holiday money too! Ten pounds, they gave me! All to myself! I'd never been so rich!

Grampy said I could find a beach ball to buy when I got to the holiday place. And a bucket and spade if I wanted. Mum said I might even be able to afford a fishing net too.

But then I had the idea of buying some scuba gear. Or a small yacht. Then, once I'd thought about it a bit more, I couldn't decide what I was going to buy.

That's the **trouble with being rich.**

There are far too many things you can afford. Especially when you're going on holiday!

Then Mum said that it would probably be best to wait until we actually got to where we were going and then decide. If we waited till we got to where we were going, I might find something else to spend my money on.

Something I hadn't thought of.

So I waited.

And waited.

And waited and waited.

About four and a half blimmin' weeks!

Chapter 3

The **trouble with waiting about four and a half blimmin' weeks to go on holiday** is it makes you go all trembly and excited. Especially when you've found out where you're going!

I thought we were going to go to Cornwall again, which is in England, so when my mum told me we were going to Spain, my eyeballs nearly popped out and rolled across the carpet!

Spain isn't even in England. It's in a completely different country of the world!

Plus, to get to Spain you can't go in your car, you have to fly there in an actual aeroplane! An actual aeroplane that takes off and flies through the actual sky and goes above the actual clouds and everything!

When I found out I was going to be going on an actual aeroplane to actual Spain for my actual summer holiday, even my trembles got the trembles!

"Now don't get over-over-excited like you normally do, Daisy," said Mum. "You know what happens when you get over-over-excited."

But I couldn't stop myself.

I rang my best friend Gabby straight away to tell her the news, but she wasn't in.

So I ran all the way, three doors up the road, to my second best friend Dylan's house to tell him instead.

Dylan has been to loads of places in the world. He is nine though. (And he's got a snake.)

Dylan told me Turkey was good, Egypt was too hot, Clacton was wicked, especially the slot machines, but Spain was definitely the best.

And guess what!

That's exactly what Gabby said when I saw her too. Not about Turkey and Egypt and Clacton, because she hadn't been there. But about Spain. Gabby had definitely been to Spain. She had photos and a Spanish teddy to prove it!

The **trouble with Spanish teddies** is they're a bit stiff. And not very cuddly. Plus they don't look like teddies, they look more like cows.

Gabby said they don't have teddies that look like teddies in Spain. They only have teddies that look like black bulls or donkeys.

Black bulls and stiff donkeys? I definitely wasn't going to spend my holiday money on a teddy like that. I was going to spend it on something much better.

Like a harpoon gun maybe. Or a jet ski!

Gabby told me that swimming pools in Spain had blow-up dolphins that you can sit on. And Spain had ice creams with gobstoppers full of bubble gum in them.

So then I got even more excited. But I still had ages to wait!

Which made me get even MORE EXCITED!!!!

Then Mum showed me a picture of the hotel where we would be staying!

And the beach we would be going to.

And the swimming pool we would be swimming in.

And the slide I would be sliding down.

And then she showed me where Spain was on the map.

And then a few days later she bought me a new swimming costume!

And the next week she bought me some new flip-flops.

And the week after that she bought me some special sun cream that would make my face turn blue!

And then the week after that it was almost time to go!

By the time we started doing the proper actual packing, my trembles were nearly shaking I was so excited!

Chapter 4

The **trouble with suitcases** is they won't shut. Not if you put too many things in them, they won't.

Mum said our suitcase would shut, but she was definitely wrong.

Even when she bounced up and down on it, our red suitcase wouldn't close.

"Sit on it with me, Daisy," she said.

So I did. But when we bounced up and down to make it close, the sun cream got squashed and squirted out all over the bed.

Luckily, it wasn't my special blue sun cream because I was going to need that for doing scary faces on holiday, but Mum still wasn't very happy.

Then she tried putting the suitcase on the floor and standing on it.

But standing on it didn't work either.

So she tried jumping on it.

But this time the handle on her hairbrush snapped, and then, when she jumped up and down the next time, the heel broke off one of her favourite shoes.

I said she didn't need eight pairs of shoes to go on holiday, but Mum said she needed a pair for every day we were going to be there, plus a pair for emergencies.

So I asked if I could take my bike for emergencies too.

But she said no.

Then she opened the suitcase and started taking all my things out! Well, not ALL my things – she left all my holiday clothes inside, but she took out all my toys. Including my roller blades and my giant super-soaker water pistol!

Mum said roller blades wouldn't work on sand, and if I wanted to super-soak someone on holiday, then I could splash them with swimming-pool water instead.

So I said some of her shoes

wouldn't work on sand either, especially the ones with high heels, plus about eight of her dresses wouldn't work on sand either.

Mum said they weren't meant to work on sand, they were meant to work on dance floors.

In the end we gave up sitting and bouncing and jumping on our red suitcase, and borrowed an extra one from Nanny and Grampy instead. Not a red one; a brown one with a squeaky wheel.

That night, Mum said I could put some extra toys in my school rucksack too, as long as I promised to carry it all the way to Spain.

That's the **trouble with carrying rucksacks**. You can never get anyone to carry them for you.

So I only put a pad in, and some comics to read on the plane.

Plus my smallest teddy.

And a smallish giraffe.

Then, once I had added my pencil case and my favourite key ring with a monkey on it, I was all packed and ready to go! Then I started to feel

really really really excited.

"Mum, can I—?"

"No, you can't stay up late," said my mum, before I'd even got a chance to finish what I was saying. "The taxi will be picking us up at three a.m. to take us to the airport tomorrow, Daisy," she told me. "I want you to have an early night tonight."

That's the trouble with my mum.

She always knows what I'm going to say next.

Well, nearly almost always.

"And can I—?"

"And can you what?" asked my mum.

"And can I sleep in my clothes?" I asked. "Please, Mum, let me sleep in my clothes. Then I'll be all ready to go on holiday the moment you wake me up!"

The **trouble with me saying "Can I?"** is nearly always my mum says no.

But guess what! This time she didn't say no, she said yes!

"Good idea, Daisy," she said. "Anything that saves time in the morning is a good idea in my books!"

"Plus please can I—?"

"Plus please can you what now?" asked Mum, with a bit of a frown on her face this time.

"Plus please can I drive the aeroplane tomorrow?" I asked.

"No you can't, Daisy," she said. "Seven-year-olds do not drive aeroplanes to Spain."

Well, it was worth a try.

Chapter 5

The **trouble with taxis** is they are always late.

It was ten past three the next morning. I had got up, eaten my breakfast, brushed my hair, cleaned my teeth, put my trainers on, zipped up my rucksack, unzipped my rucksack (to check my monkey key ring was in there), zipped up my rucksack again, unzipped it again (to check I'd put a rubber in my pencil case), zipped it up again, unzipped it again (to talk to my teddy), zipped it up again, put my jacket on, put my rucksack on my back, taken my rucksack off my back (to see if my monkey key ring was still there), put my rucksack on again, walked round and round the lounge at least fifteen times, and the taxi STILL hadn't arrived!

Mum was starting to get a bit fidgety too, but just as she picked up the phone to find out where it was, the taxi pulled up outside our house.

"At last!" she said. "Come on, Daisy, it's time to go!"

The taxi driver got out of his car to help Mum with the suitcases.

It was really dark and exciting outside our house. Everyone in the whole street was asleep except for me and Mum! Even the birds were still asleep!

When we drove past Dylan's house, I looked up at his bedroom curtains and imagined him snoring in his bed. Then I imagined his pet snake Shooter curled up on his heat pads too.

Being the only one awake in the street was reeeeeeally exciting!

When we got to a bigger road, we saw that other people in England were awake too. Not many, but at least twelve. I asked my mum if she thought they were all going on a summer holiday too. She said that some might be, but most were probably going to work or coming home from work.

I didn't know people went to do jobs that early in the morning. Or came home from them that late.

Mum said that milkmen do very early jobs, so that when they put the milk on your doorstep, they can make sure it's nice and fresh.

That's the **trouble with milk** – if you don't keep it fresh it goes all lumpy and mouldy.

And it smells. I sniffed some

mouldy milk when I was round at Gabby's house once, and both our noses nearly fell off it was so stinky.

Now we only sniff nice things. Like Playdoh.

The **trouble with my mum at half-past three in the morning** is she doesn't want to play games or anything.

I thought playing games in the taxi would be really exciting, but Mum just said that she was too tired.

Then she said, "Daisy, we've got a long day ahead. Why don't you close your eyes and try and get some more sleep before we get to the airport?"

SLEEP? When you're going to AN AIRPORT? How could anyone possibly sleep when they are in an actual taxi, going to an actual airport with an actual aeroplane that's going to fly you all the way to ACTUAL SPAIN?!!!!

I couldn't even close my eyes!

So I played I-Spy on my own.

The **trouble with playing I-Spy on your own** is you always know the answers.

So I counted lampposts instead.

The **trouble** **with** **counting** **lampposts** is there are too many, so I counted horses instead.

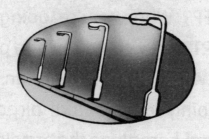

The **trouble with counting horses** is there weren't any, so I imagined I was Spanish instead.

The **trouble with imagining you're Spanish** is it's really hard if you haven't been to Spain before.

I could imagine where I lived. I lived in a smallish castle with palm trees and coconuts in the garden. It was very hot, the sun was always shining and the sky was really blue, but my face was even bluer because of my sun cream. I had two pets. My black bull was called Blackie and my donkey was called Giddyup.

Plus my name wasn't Daisy – it was Daisyella, because in Spain children are only allowed to have Spanish-sounding names.

My best friends were called Gabbyella instead of Gabby and Pepe instead of Dylan.

My favourite food was sausagellas with tomatoella sauce.

My favourite drink was fizzy orangella and my favourite crisps were smoky baconella.

But after that I couldn't think of anything else Spanish, so I watched my mum dribbling instead.

The **trouble with dribble** is it always comes out when you're asleep.

I don't know why, because if you go to sleep, then your dribble should go to sleep too really.

But it doesn't. At least my mum's dribble doesn't. My mum's dribble goes really dribbly when she's asleep. Especially when she starts snoring.

The **trouble with snoring** is when they get to be big snores, they sound like a pig eating porridge.

And they make your dribble wobble.

I thought the taxi driver might crash the car when Mum started dribbling AND snoring so I gave her a nudge with my elbow.

The **trouble with nudging someone with your elbow** is it makes them jump if they're asleep. And it makes their dribble go all over their face.

Mum wiped her dribble off really quickly, sat up straight and pretended she hadn't been asleep in the first place.

But I could see her eyes closing again in the reflection in the taxi window. So I didn't nudge her again after that. Not until we arrived at the airport.

Chapter 6

The **trouble with arriving at airports** is it's really hard not to jump up and down! Even if you've got your seat belt on!

Arriving at airports is so exciting! All the buildings are big and square and made out of concrete. And all the lights are really bright. Plus there are absolutely loads of people everywhere.

Plus if you look up in the sky, you can see actual planes coming in to land and other ones that are taking off! You should see how big aeroplanes look when they are close up! I thought one was going to land on our head!

When we got out of our taxi, there were people pushing trolleys into the airport and people pushing trolleys out of the airport all over the place! All the people going in had long trousers on but some of the people coming out were wearing shorts! And flip-flops! And they had suntans and everything!

Mum said the people coming out of the airport had been on their holidays and the people going in were about to start their holidays.

Just like us!

After Mum had paid the taxi man, we went and got a trolley all of our own!

The **trouble with trolleys all of your own** is they make you want to have a ride on them.

Mum said you aren't really meant to ride on trolleys at the airport in case you fall off, but once we'd put our suitcases on, she let me climb on top!

It was brilliant!!!!

Then guess what we had to do! We had to go through some really big

turning doors! Not normal doors like you get at home, but great big ones that turned round and round like a roundabout. It was so much fun, Mum and me went round in circles three times before we went in!

And then guess what!

We had to go along a really long piece of floor that actually moved! It was just like moving carpet, except it wasn't made of carpet. It was black like rubber. Anyway, you didn't have to walk on it or anything. All you had to do was stand on it and it carried you all the way inside!

I'd never seen inside an airport before. It was amazing!

I'd never seen so many people

before either. Or trolleys! Or suitcases! Or queues! There were queues everywhere. Really long ones too.

It took us ages to get our passports looked at, and ages to get our suitcases weighed, and ages to get our tickets from the lady, but I didn't care. We were in an ACTUAL AIRPORT, going to ACTUAL SPAIN on an ACTUAL SUMMER HOLIDAY for SEVEN WHOLE ACTUAL DAYS!!!!!

I'd have queued for a hundred years to do that! (I don't think Mum would have though.)

That's the **trouble with queues**. You have to be quite small to enjoy them.

It's the same with airport floors.

The **trouble with airport floors** is they make you want to do skids.

Once we'd done all our queuing I just had to do some big skids! Mum said I shouldn't do skids in airports because I might knock someone over or crash into a trolley, but I couldn't stop myself. One skid I did went about five metres! (That was a standing-up skid.)

Another one I did went about seven and a half metres. (That was a skidding-on-my-knees skid.)

But then the next skid I did went straight into a man carrying a cup of coffee.

I didn't go very far on that one, but his coffee did.

His coffee went about eleven metres. All over the floor. And down his shirt.

That's the **trouble with people who drink coffee.** They're always drinking it where children need to do skids.

So I had to stop doing skids after that.

And I had to say sorry.

Plus my mum had to buy the

man another coffee. But not another shirt.

She did offer to buy him another shirt, but the man said he would be fine when he had dried out. And anyway, it serves him right really, for not looking where he was going.

Chapter 7

The **trouble with x-ray machines** is people aren't allowed to lie down and go through them.

I wanted my mum to lie down and go through the x-ray machine. That way I would have been able to see her being a skeleton!

That's what x-ray machines do. They see right through the outside of

things and show you all the bits on
the inside.

Mum said we were only allowed to
put our bags and jackets and shoes
through the x-ray machines.

But the **trouble with bags and jackets and shoes** is they don't have skeletons in the middle. Which means they're not as good.

Once we'd put our bags on the x-ray machine we had to walk through a special rectangle that bleeped if you were carrying daggers or machine guns or swords or key rings with monkeys on.

When I went bleep, I thought I was going to be arrested and sent to prison or something, but when the x-ray man found my key ring in my pocket he let me go free.

Which is lucky really because prison is nowhere near as good as Spain.

After I'd stopped bleeping, my mum made me put my monkey key ring in my rucksack, and then we went to the airport shops. I couldn't wait to spend my holiday money!

The **trouble with airport shops** is most of them don't have scuba gear in them.

Or small yachts.

Mum said that if I saw anything else in the shops that I wanted to spend my holiday money on, I should let her know.

But I couldn't see any harpoon guns or jet skis or ice creams with bubble gum in them either.

I did see a strawberry Cornetto that looked quite nice, but Mum said I wasn't allowed ice cream at six o'clock in the morning.

I wasn't allowed an underwater wristwatch either. Or a basketball net.

In the end I decided to save my

holiday money until I got to Spain. Which was lucky really, because I didn't know at the time that I would need it for the kittens.

The **trouble with seats in airport lounges** is when you try and lie across three seats at once, the gaps in between make you feel all uncomfortable.

Mum said I should sit up nicely and listen for our plane to be announced.

But other people were lying all over the seats. And they were grown-ups! One man with knots in his hair and a giant rucksack was lying across about six seats! So I didn't see why I couldn't.

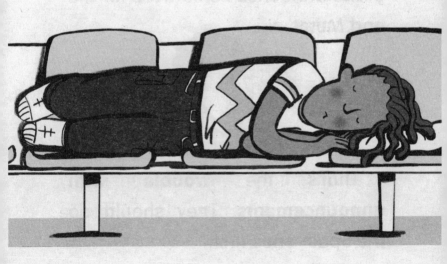

Except I thought I'd fall through the gaps, so I did sit up in the end.

The **trouble with airport announcers** is they always say the wrong plane. Loads of planes were taking off all the time to loads of holidays all over the world. But none of the announcements were for me and Mum!

That's the **trouble with announcements.** They should do the Spain ones first.

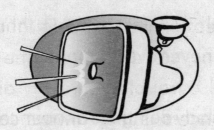

Mum told me that our flight number was MLG452 and that as soon as our plane had been cleaned and tidied and filled up with petrol, then there would be an announcement for us to get on our plane too.

I said I didn't mind going to Spain in a dirty plane or one that didn't have much petrol in it, but Mum said that wasn't a very good idea.

So we waited.

And waited and waited.

Until . . . just when I thought it would never ever happen . . .

IT DID!

The lady doing the announcements actually announced our actual plane to actual Spain!

"Time to go, Daisy!" said Mum. "We need to go to gate fifty-three. Gate fifty-three is where our plane will be taking off from soon!"

The **trouble with gate fifty-threes** is they feel like they are about fifty-three miles from the airport!

Mum said it was nothing like fifty-three miles away, but it felt like ever such a long walk to me.

That's the **trouble with small legs**. They start to ache much earlier than longer ones. Especially if you're carrying a rucksack.

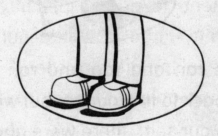

Except that's when I realized I wasn't!

I wasn't carrying my rucksack at all!

I'D LEFT MY RUCKSACK UNDER THE SEAT IN THE AIRPORT LOUNGE!!!

The **trouble with leaving rucksacks under seats in airport lounges** is you're not allowed to do it.

We ran and ran and ran all the way back to the lounge, but when we got to our seat, there were about five policemen moving people away from my school bag!!!!!

At first I thought someone had tried to steal my monkey key ring, but then

Mum went really red and said that the policemen were checking inside my school bag for a bomb!

The **trouble with bombs** is they can blow up, so I would never EVER put one in my school bag. Plus I don't know where to buy bombs.

Mum knew that, because she's my mum, but the policemen hadn't met me before so she had to tell them. Which made her go even redder than red.

At first the policemen did loads of frowns at her, then, before they gave me my rucksack back, they checked my mum for bombs too!

In front of loads and loads of people.

Mum said she'd never been so embarrassed in her life. Which is probably true.

Then there was another announcement. Except this time it didn't say the name of our aeroplane – it said OUR names instead! In big loud words right across the airport!

"QUICK, DAISY!" said Mum. "IT'S OUR LAST CALL! Run as fast as you can or we're going to MISS OUR PLANE!"

The **trouble with missing your plane** is it means you will miss your holiday too!

So we had to run all the way!

The **trouble with running all the way to gate fifty-three** is it makes your legs ache EVEN MORE! Plus it makes your face all hot and red, and your back all sticky.

By the time we got there, my mum could hardly speak she was so out of breath!

Plus her face was a new kind of red I'd never ever seen before.

"DON'T EVER LEAVE A BAG UNATTENDED IN AN AIRPORT AGAIN, DAISY!" was all she could manage to say.

"I'M SO EXCITED, I'M SO EXCITED, I'M SO EXCITED!!!" was all I could say back.

Chapter 8

The **trouble with aeroplanes** is all the seats should be by the windows. If all the seats in aeroplanes were by the windows, then everyone could look out.

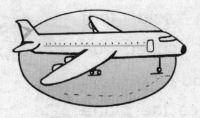

Mum said she didn't mind not looking out of the window because she'd looked out of an aeroplane window before, but I think putting seats in the middle of an aeroplane is silly.

Before we put our seat belts on we had to put our bags in a high-up cupboard above our seats.

Mum said that it was called an overhead locker and that once the plane had taken off, she would get my things out of my rucksack to play with.

Then we had to put our seat belts on.

The **trouble with seat belts** is you're not allowed to keep unclipping them and then doing them up again, and then unclipping them and doing them up again.

I got really good at undoing and doing up my seat belt, but then I got frowned at by an aeroplane lady. Then my mum said the plane wouldn't take off if I didn't leave my seat belt alone.

So I had to just do it up and not unclip it after that.

When we took off, my tummy went all funny. That's the **trouble with planes taking off** – they go so fast, your tummy can't keep up.

At first I nearly didn't look out of the window, but when I did it was brilliant! Everything on the ground had gone really small!

All the cars on the roads looked

like teensy toy ones and all the trees and fields looked like tiny broccolis inside little green squares.

Mum said the higher we got, the smaller everything would look.

And she was right, because then we went even higher! We went right up up up into the air above the actual clouds! Real ACTUAL clouds! Great big, fat, fluffy ones that looked like great big, fat oodles and oodles of white, fluffy cotton wool.

I wanted to get out of the plane and bounce about on them, but Mum said no one was allowed outside during the journey.

And anyway, we still had to keep our seat belts on.

That's the **trouble with seat belts**. If you take them off before you're allowed to, the aeroplane lady will come and tell you off.

When we were allowed to undo our seat belts, the captain driving the plane did an announcement. He said that we would soon be cruising at 37,000 feet and that a little bit later we were going to be given breakfast to eat, plus teas and coffees!

Then I decided I needed my pad and pencil case.

The **trouble with needing a pad and pencil case when they're in an overhead locker** is your mum has to undo her seat belt, get up, squeeze past the person she's sitting next to, reach up to the overhead cupboard and take the pad and pencil case out of your bag to give it to you.

The **trouble with needing a comic just after you've needed a pad and pencil case** is then your mum has to do it all over again.

Then I needed my giraffe. And then I needed my monkey key ring.

Which made her a little bit cross and the person she was sitting next to a little bit huffy and puffy.

So in the end Mum took my whole rucksack down from the overhead locker, gave it to me and told me to keep it under the seat in front of me.

So I did.

But then I needed to go to the loo.

The **trouble with loos on aeroplanes** is they are a bit small.

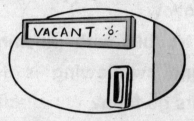

My loo at home has a bath in it and everything. The one on our aeroplane didn't even have a shower. Or EVEN a rubber duck!

Plus when I was sitting on the loo seat, my ears began to feel all shushy.

When I came out of the loo, my mum said that because we were so high up in the sky, the air pressure in our ears could begin to feel different. Then she told me to pinch my nose and swallow.

The **trouble with pinching your nose and swallowing** is it makes your ears go funny.

At first I didn't know what my ears were doing. They just felt wiggly inside and then everything went all loud.

Mum said it was called popping. But I didn't really like it.

I preferred not popping, or still shushy.

When we got back to our seats, I got my pad and pencils out of my bag to do some drawing.

"Draw an aeroplane," said Mum. "Draw a Spanish aeroplane."

Which was quite a good idea.

Except by then I'd worked out how to play with the tray in my seat.

The **trouble with aeroplane trays when they're right in front of you** is they really make you want to lower them and then push them up again.

And then lower them and push them up again.

And lower them and push them up again.

And lower them and push them up again.

Because it's really good fun.

Trouble is, the man sitting in the seat in front of me didn't know how to work his tray. So he got all jealous and huffy and puffy, and kept turning round to frown at me.

So Mum said I had better put my tray up and leave it up.

But I couldn't, because our breakfast had arrived!

Chapter 9

The **trouble with breakfasts on aeroplanes** is they don't do Coco Pops. They do sort-of-sausage and sort-of-bacon with sort-of-baked beans with sort-of-potatoes in a white plastic tray instead.

At first I didn't know what sort of breakfast it would be because I couldn't get the foil lid off, but when Mum pulled it off for me, I could see it wasn't Coco Pops.

So I just had my bread roll and orange juice instead.

Mum said that they probably wouldn't have Coco Pops in Spain either, and that not having Coco Pops on the plane would be good practice for not having Coco Pops in the hotel.

And she was right. Our hotel in Spain didn't do Coco Pops either.

But they did do Rice Krispies.

And they did kittens!

Not for breakfast. Just for stroking.

You should never put milk on kittens. It's all right to put milk in their saucer for them to drink, but you mustn't pour it actually on them.

Or sprinkle sugar on them.

Pouring milk or sprinkling sugar on kittens isn't allowed in Spain. Or any country in the world.

Otherwise you'll go to prison.

But stroking them is definitely all right. And cuddling them.

But playing with them is EVEN better!!!! If you ask me, playing with kittens is one of the best things you can do in the world.

Honestly, if I'd known there were going to be kittens at our hotel in Spain, I wouldn't have put any toys in my rucksack to play with AT ALL! Not even my monkey key ring!

I mean, who needs toys and teddies and key rings and colouring pens and pads in your rucksack when you've got kittens to play with?

NO ONE. That's who!

Still, at least the things in my rucksack gave me something to do on the plane.

I was going to play I-Spyella with Mum. I-Spyella is a new Spanish I-Spy game I have invented, but the trouble was, by the time I had drawn a Spanish aeroplane and some Spanish clouds and some really really high-up Spanish seagulls, my mum had fallen asleep and started snoring again.

Then she started dribbling again. Which I'm not sure is allowed on planes.

Luckily the aeroplane lady who gave us our breakfast didn't see the dribble, or she might have told the captain. And then the captain might have told everyone in the plane in an announcement!

"This is your captain speaking. We have a dribble alert in seat fourteen B. Please be careful that you don't get dribbled on when you walk past seat fourteen B, because the lady who is snoring next to the little girl in seat fourteen A is dribbling all over the place."
Or something like that.

That's the **trouble with dribble alerts.** They can be really embarrassing. Especially if you're not allowed to jump off the plane.

Which you're definitely not.

Unless you've got a parachute.

So I just stayed quiet in my seat, played with my toys and coloured with my colouring pens.

While my mum dribbled.

Alllllllllllllllllllllllllllllllllllll

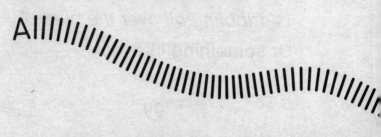

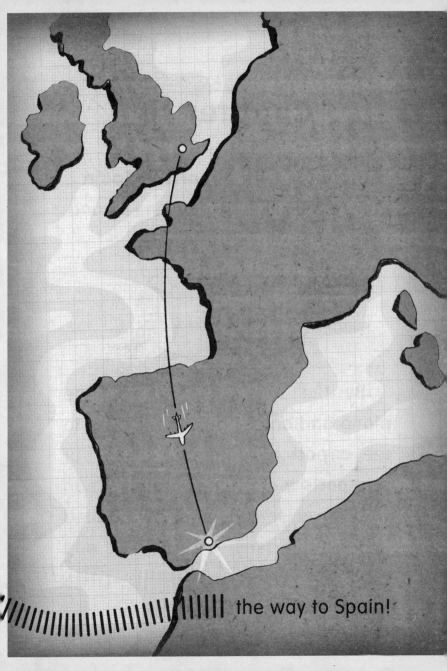

the way to Spain!

Chapter 10

The **trouble with airports in Spain** is they're a bit like the ones in England. Only hotter.

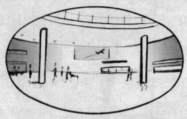

By the time we'd got off the plane and onto a bus, and driven to the airport building and given our passports to a grumpy Spanish man who never smiled, and then waited for our suitcases to come out, and

then found a trolley, and then lifted my rucksack onto the trolley, and then gone back to try and find Nanny and Grampy's squeaky-wheel, my face was really boiling!

That's the **trouble with sunshine in Spain.** It can burn straight through whole buildings!

And coaches!

The coach that drove us to our hotel after we'd left the airport was even hotter!

Mum said that the air conditioning on the coach can't have been working, and that if we were going to have a holiday in Spain, then we would just have to get used to hot temperatures.

If you ask me, my mum was really pleased it was so hot in Spain. Being hot in Spain makes the dribble on your shoulder dry up much much quicker.

It was faaaaaaaaar too hot in the coach for me though. Sitting on that coach was like being a jacket potato in a microwave. No, it was like being a chicken nugget in a red-hot oven.

Actually it was like being a crispy sausage that's fallen through the gap onto the barbecue coals, and then had loads more red-hot coals and some burning mustard put on top.

Anyway, that's probably why I fainted.

Mum said I didn't faint. I fell asleep.

But I definitely didn't.

Even if she said I did.

And I definitely didn't do any snoring.

Even if she said I did.

And I definitely didn't do any DRIBBLING!

Even Mum said I didn't do any dribbling. Anyway . . . BOY was I pleased when we arrived at our hotel!

And DOUBLE BOY was I excited when we got our suitcases off the coach and carried them inside!

You should have seen how Spanish everything was inside the hotel. Everywhere I looked there were Spanish things all over the place! There were Spanish people with Spanish name badges, there were great big Spanish pots with blue and white patterns on them, and massive posters of Spanish ladies doing Spanish dancing on the wall, plus there was a great big Spanish floor that you could do Spanish skids on, plus there were actual plants with lemons growing on them in actual Spanish . . . and you'll just never guess what else there was – growing out of the actual ground INSIDE the actual hotel – you'll just never guess . . .

Right up close to where we were actually standing!

And over by the window.

And over by all the other windows too!

There were real actual Spanish palm trees all over the place!

I reckon someone must have picked all the coconuts, because I couldn't see any, but all the other palm-tree bits were there! Great big trunks and great big palm-tree leaves, GROWING INSIDE our actual hotel!!

It was so exciting, I wanted to jump up and down and do skids and roly-polys all over the place! I wanted to do whoop-de-doops and fiddle-de-dellas and be jumpier and skiddier than I'd ever been before in my whole life!!!

And then I realized why!

I'd never been excited in Spanish before!

Mum said I should remember that I was English and try and keep my whoop-de-doops and fiddle-de-dellas to a minimum.

So I tried.

But then I saw our room!

And then I saw our balcony!

And then I saw the pool!

I could see the actual swimming pool from the actual balcony of our actual room!!!!

It had really blue water with people in it, plus a great big YELLOW SLIDE!

I've never put a swimming costume on so fast in my life!

Chapter 11

The **trouble with swimming costumes** is after you put them on you have to put sun cream on AS WELL.

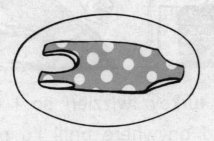

ALL THE TIME!

I couldn't wait to get into the pool and slide down the great big yellow slide into the water, but Mum said midday suns in Spain can roast you

like a turkey twizzler, so I wasn't allowed anywhere until I'd put my sun cream on.

The first time my mum put the sun cream on my face, I asked her to do me a really scary zombie face so I could frighten everyone in the pool.

Trouble is, when I got to the pool, lots of other children had scary blue zombie faces too!

One boy called Harrison even had a green face! Harrison was the first friend I met in the pool on holiday.

Actually, I didn't exactly meet him, I kind of landed on top of him. Which wasn't my fault, because he shouldn't have been doing shark impressions at the bottom of the yellow slide.

And anyway, it didn't hurt him when I landed on him. He just went under the water, disappeared for a while and then came up over by the getting-out steps.

Except he didn't get out, he stayed in.

At first I thought he might be a bit cross, but he wasn't cross at all. He smiled at me, emptied some water out of his swimming goggles, and then swam back towards me to say hello.

Harrison was eight, and ever such a good swimmer. And he could do proper dives into the deep end with his legs together. Plus he had a baby sister called Jo-Jo.

The **trouble with Jo-Jo** is she was only three, which meant she sank nearly all the time. Unless she had her rubber ring and armbands on.

Harrison said he was in charge of Jo-Jo when she was in the pool, especially when his mum and dad were lying down on the sun loungers with their eyes shut. Which was most of the time.

Harrison said that being in charge of Jo-Jo was the same as being a lifeguard, which is really good, because I'd never met an actual lifeguard before. Especially a green one!

When Harrison took me over to the shallow end to meet Jo-Jo, I met loads of other children on the way.

There was Carly, who was from Birmingham, Danny from Newcastle, Matty from Devon, and Cerise and Montague from Surrey. Cerise and Montague were really tanned because they'd already been at the hotel for a week.

Everyone else was mostly blue, except for Matty, who was blue with pink-and-red peely bits on his shoulders.

Everyone wanted to play with me, and everyone wanted to know my name. It was brilliant. I'd only been in the pool five minutes and I had seven new friends already!

Harrison and Jo-Jo were going to be my best friends on holiday though.

I'd never have found the kittens without Harrison and Jo-Jo. At least, not without Harrison and Jo-Jo's Frisbee.

Chapter 12

The **trouble with Frisbees** is you can never be *exactly* sure where they are going to go.

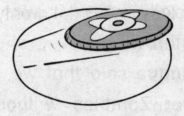

Every afternoon straight after lunch, me, Harrison, Matty, Carly, Cerise and Montague would meet by the slide with our T-shirts on, and then play Zombie Mermaids in the pool. Trouble is, boys don't usually want to be mermaids, even when they are zombie ones, so we couldn't really play Zombie Mermaids for very long.

Everyone wanted to play Frisbee-throwing though!

Especially when it was zombie Frisbee-throwing!

Montague said that we could all be Water Zombies (without being mermaids), and that our special zombie Frisbee was made out of red-hot lava. Which meant if you held it for too long all your fingers would melt off and sink to the bottom of the pool!

The **trouble with your fingers sinking to the bottom of the pool** is you can't hold Spanish lemonade or ice cream or anything, so if the Frisbee came to you, you had to throw it to someone else really fast!

The **trouble with throwing Frisbees really fast** is they can almost go into space. Especially if you're not standing in the pool when you throw it.

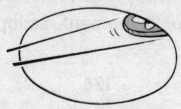

I did start off in the pool, and even when I was right up to my shoulders in water, I did some really good throws.

Trouble is, then I found a beetle floating in the water beside me.

Matty said it was a zombie headlouse from Deadland, but it wasn't. It was definitely a shiny black-and-green beetle from Spain. It splashed straight towards me and even touched my arm.

AND . . . its legs were still moving!

So I had to stop playing Zombie Frisbee for a moment, scoop it into a plastic cup and throw it out of the pool back onto the concrete.

The **trouble with throwing beetles out of swimming pools** is they land upside down!

The **trouble with beetles landing upside down** is then they can't turn themselves the right way up. They just stay upside down and wriggle and wriggle and wriggle. At least Spanish beetles do.

So I had to get out of the pool to help turn it over.

The **trouble with turning beetles over** is you can't really do it with your fingers. In case they nip you.

So you have to find a lolly stick to turn them over with instead. Then, once you've found a lolly stick, you have to concentrate really hard on getting the beetle's legs to grab on.

Which is quite hard.

And then you have to turn him over without him letting go.

Or he might fall off and land upside down again.

Which is even harder.

So when a zombie Frisbee comes to you, you don't really notice it at first.

And then, when everyone screams "Zombie Fingers!" at you, it really makes you jump.

And when you look round at everyone in the pool and they're telling you you've only got two seconds before your fingers melt off, it makes you really panic, pick up the zombie Frisbee and throw it away REALLY fast . . .

So fast that it goes right across the pool, straight over the sun loungers, in between some palm trees and over a fence.

Which wasn't my fault.

Except everyone said it was.

At first they laughed and splashed about and said it was really funny. Carly said I must have done a Turbo

Zombie Frisbee throw, Matty said I must have switched to Zombie Space Catapult Force, and Cerise said I'd thrown it so hard she was surprised my arm hadn't fallen off and landed in the pool! Which was the funniest.

But then Montague said I had to go and get the Frisbee back from over the fence. Which is wrong, because it wasn't even his Frisbee in the first place. It was Harrison and Jo-Jo's.

Then EVERYONE said I had to go and get the Frisbee back from over the fence, including Harrison and Jo-Jo. Because I was the one who had thrown it over.

Plus I was already out of the pool. (Thanks to that beetle!)

So I had no choice. I HAD to go and look for the Frisbee. Which meant I had to go behind the fence too.

The **trouble with fences** is they can be a bit strange when they're Spanish. Especially when you don't know what is on the other side.

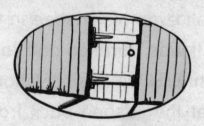

So I asked Montague and Cerise to come with me.

But they wouldn't. Montague said

that his flip-flops were under the bed in his hotel room and that Spanish concrete was too hot for his feet.

Cerise said she wanted to have a go on the slide, Matty said he wanted to practise his duck diving, Carly said she was feeling a bit sunburned (which was definitely a lie, because she was bluer than any of us), and Danny said he needed to check the battery on his iPod.

Not including Jo-Jo, that only left Harrison.

I knew Harrison wouldn't let me down!

Chapter 13

The moment I saw the kittens I knew this was going to be my best holiday ever! Harrison said he saw them first because he was the first one to go through the gate in the fence. But he definitely didn't see them first.

He saw the Frisbee first, but it was me who saw the kittens. They were curled up under a bush beside some big metal dustbins.

The dustbins were really smelly and had Spanish flies buzzing all round them. But I didn't care. I only

cared about the kittens.

There were five! A grey one, a grey-and-white one, a black one, a black-and-white one and a ginger one! And there was a mummy one! The mummy one was kind of tabby coloured with a white tip on her tail. She was really skinny and, at first when she saw me, she looked a bit scared.

But when she realized I could do Spanish cat-talk, she was all right.

The **trouble with Spanish cat-talk** is only me and Spanish cats and kittens can understand it.

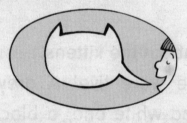

Harrison didn't understand it, and neither did Jo-Jo when we showed her the kittens the next day.

Spanish cat-talk is a mixture of sign language and squeaks. You either know how to do it or you don't. Which was a shame for Harrison and Jo-Jo because they didn't know how to do it, but then Harrison and Jo-Jo aren't as good with animals as I am.

Which is why it was better if I was more in charge of the kittens than them.

Even if Harrison was older than me.

Harrison said he definitely understood why the kittens had made their nest under a bush beside the dustbins. He said dustbins were full of things to eat, and so being next to one would mean they could always get food anytime they wanted it.

Which isn't true.

Because the **trouble with Spanish dustbins** is kittens can't get the lids off. Neither can mummy cats. Because the lids are too heavy and high up.

Which is probably why the kittens looked so skinny too. Especially the littlest black one.

I was the first one to touch her. She was soooooooooooo CUTE!

I was a bit nervous at first in case the mummy cat tried to scratch me. But after I'd squeaked to explain that I was only going to be kind to her kittens, and that later on I would come back and give them some food, she let me crouch down beside the bush, put my hand in and stroke them.

Then she even let me pick up one of her kittens!

The **trouble with picking up a Spanish kitten** is other people always want to have a hold too.

I'd only had the black one in the palm of my hand for about ten seconds before Harrison said it was his turn to hold him now.

So I had to let him. Otherwise it wouldn't have been fair.

Harrison said he thought he might have suddenly found the powers

to speak Spanish cat-talk, but he definitely hadn't.

Harrison's squeaks didn't sound like Spanish cat-language at all.

They sounded more like Russian hamster-language, if you ask me.

But I didn't tell him that. Because that wouldn't have been very fair either. Or kind.

So at first I only got a little hold of the black kitten.

And no holds of the other kittens at all!

Because before I could reach under the bush to get another one, Angelo came out of the back door of the pool bar and found us over by the dustbins.

Angelo is my favourite Spanish waiter in the world. He was really nice and friendly to us all the time we were on holiday. But the first time he met us, he said children weren't allowed around the dustbins, and he would get told off if he didn't ask us to leave.

Which I don't think was true either.

If you ask me, the reason he wanted us to go back to the pool had nothing to do with the dustbins. If you ask me, Angelo just wanted us

to go so he could smoke a cigarette without anyone seeing.

I'm definite about it actually, because I saw him hide a cigarette behind his back when he saw us. Plus when he asked us our names, there was smoke coming up from over his shoulder.

The **trouble with smoking cigarettes** is they can kill you. Whatever language you smoke them in, they can kill you deader than dead.

Cigarettes have got bad stuff inside them that can clog up your whole body and stop you breathing. And they can turn your teeth yellow.

And your hair.

My mum says that my granddad, who died before I was born, used to smoke, and the front of his hair went really yellow. Then he got a smoking disease and he died.

Like my dad.

Except my dad didn't die of smoke.

Or cigarettes.

He died of a car crash. When I was little.

But I don't remember. I've never remembered.

I hardly remember anything about when I was little.

I will remember never ever to smoke though.

Not in English or Spanish or any language. Which is why I had to tell Angelo off.

When Angelo found out Harrison and I had seen his cigarette, he dropped it on the ground and squashed the smoke out of it with the heel of his shoe.

Then he promised us he would never ever smoke a cigarette again. So we decided to like him. And he decided to like us!

It was Angelo who told us that the Spanish word for "never ever" was "no way José".

And that the Spanish word for kittens was *"gatitos"*!

It was Angelo who told us that the kittens were about ten weeks old, and that they had actually been born under the actual bush beside the actual dustbins!

It was Angelo who told us that he didn't know where the daddy cat was, and that Spanish daddy cats weren't very good at looking after kittens.

And it was Angelo who told us to keep the kittens a secret when we went back to the pool to play with our friends.

He said that if lots of children found out there were kittens behind the fence, then they would all want to see them and stroke them and pick them up and everything.

Then he would end up with lots of children around the dustbins.

Which meant he REALLY would get into trouble.

Plus the mummy cat might not like it.

Which meant he would have to lock the gate in the fence for good. Which meant we wouldn't be able to open it. Which meant we would never see the kittens again! Never ever!

So Harrison and me decided there and then: when we got back to the pool with the Frisbee, the five little Spanish *gatitos* behind the fence would be our five little secrets.

We wouldn't tell absolutely ANYONE about the cute little *gatitos* AT ALL! (Except for Jo-Jo and my mum.)

Chapter 14

The **trouble with my mum** is she gets jealous.

Not about kittens. About me having so many new friends.

Before I'd even got back into the pool with the Frisbee, she called me over to see her.

At first I thought she was going to tell me off for going behind a Spanish fence with Harrison, but what she had to say was much worse than that.

I couldn't believe it. Just because I'd made fourteen new friends on holiday (seven normal ones, six furry ones and Angelo), my mum decided she wanted to make a new friend too.

His name was Derek.

And he was a man.

The **trouble with men** is they might try to be my mum's boyfriend.

Which is yuk because my mum goes all different when she might be getting a boyfriend.

And she puts more make-up on.

The **trouble with my mum putting more make-up on** is it stops boyfriends from seeing how old she is in real life.

If you ask me, my mum is far too old to go out with a boyfriend. In fact, if you ask me, my mum is far too old to go out at all.

Except with me.

Like to the zoo or the shops.

Mum said that I was being silly, and that Derek and she were just good friends.

She said she had met him at the pool bar the day before. She said that Derek was very charming and very nice and would very much like to meet me!

I still didn't really want to meet him though.

I'd much rather have gone to dinner with the kittens.

Then Mum told me I HAD to meet Derek! In fact she'd already

made a date with him!

On Thursday night . . . which was only THREE days away!

Without even asking me first!

I was so cross, I nearly didn't tell her about the kittens.

And when I did tell her about the kittens, guess what she said next! She said that they sounded very nice, and that I should put on my best skirt and top when we went to dinner with Derek.

Which made me even crosser! One minute I was talking about the kittens and now we were talking about Derek again!

So I went and sat under a different umbrella.

How could she!

Just when I'd gone and found the best things I'd ever found in my life, she had to go and start putting on more make-up.

I was so cross, I could hardly think of any names to call the kittens at all!

Every time I tried to think of a really good kitten name, the name Derek kept coming into my head instead!

Derek, Derek, Derek, Derek and Derek.

Then I got so boiling cross, I had to go and jump in the pool to cool down.

Luckily the pool water really helped a lot. So did Harrison, once he'd told the others he wasn't playing Frisbee any more.

Miffy, Marble, Midnight, Mini Moo and Smoky. That's what the kittens' names would be!

Chapter 15

When Mum and me went for our
dinner in the hotel that evening, the
only thing I could think about was
the kittens. They were soooo small
and soooo skinny and soooo hungry
and soooo under–a-bush-beside-a-
dustbin . . . I just HAD to get them
something really nice to eat.

That's why I took loads of octopus
and anchovies from the buffet.

Anchovies are like tiny little fishes
in slimy sauce, just right for growing
kittens, and octopus is like . . .

Well, little bobbly bits of, er . . . octopus just right for growing kittens too.

At least Harrison said they would be, when we were standing with our plates in the buffet queue.

Harrison said he reckoned cats would absolutely love octopus and anchovies because they were made of fish. But then he said that he wouldn't actually be able to put any on his plate because his mum and dad would get suspicious.

That's the **trouble with octopus and anchovies**. Children can't eat them without looking suspicious.

Which meant my mum would be suspicious of my octopus and anchovies too.

So I hid them under a big pile of lettuce!

When I sat down at my table with a great big pile of lettuce, my mum's eyes nearly popped out of her head.

"What on earth have you got there, Daisy?" she asked.

"I fancied a lettuce salad," I said.

"A LETTUCE SALAD?" she said. "A LETTUCE BLOOMING SALAD?!" she said.

"HELLO, DEREK," she said.

That's when I met Derek for the first time.

Actually I was quite pleased to meet him because he took my mum's mind right off my lettuce.

"How are you, Derek?" said my mum, jiggling her earrings with the back of her hand and then fluttering her make-up at him like a soppy person.

"Daisy meet Derek, Derek meet Daisy," she said.

The **trouble with extra-long nostril hairs** is they make you look like a troll.

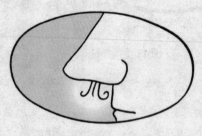

The **trouble with even medium-sized ear hairs** is they make you look like you've escaped from a zoo.

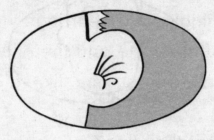

Apart from that, Derek didn't look too bad. His hair was a bit grey, his nose was a bit big, but his teeth were quite straight and he had a quite nice watch on.

Except then he did a wink.

The **trouble with winks** is strangers think they will make children like them.

Except they don't.

As far as I'm concerned, any stranger who winks at me is a total idiot.

"I believe I am going to have the pleasure of taking you and your lovely mum to dinner, Daisy," said Derek, stretching his arm across my anchovies for a handshake.

The **trouble with handshakes** is they don't work with one hand.

So I had to give him *my* hand to shake.

After we'd done the shake, Derek did ANOTHER wink!

Then he put his other hand on my mum's shoulder and whispered, "Are we still all right for Thursday?"

Then my mum went all soppy again and said that we couldn't wait

to go out for dinner with him.

Which was a lie.

"Where would you like to go?" asked Derek. "I know a lovely little Spanish tappers bar by the sea front."

"That would be lovely, Derek!" said my mum.

Which was another lie. In fact, the last thing on earth I wanted to do on my holiday was go Spanish tapping with Derek. Whatever Spanish tapping is.

"Thursday it is then!" said Derek, winking at me for a THIRD TIME, and then leaving us alone.

Nostril hairs, ear hairs and three winks!!! There was no way I was going to like Derek!

"Do we haaaaaaaave to go???" I said, hoping that my mum would change her mind and never see Derek again.

"Yes, we do haaaaaaaave to

go," said Mum. "Derek is a perfectly lovely man, and we will have a perfectly lovely evening with him on Thursday."

Except we didn't.

THANKS TO THE KITTENS!

Chapter 16

Apart from Derek and his winks, our holiday just got better and better after I'd found the kittens!

Well, mine did. Mum says hers just got worse and worse.

I used my special Spanish cat-talk to find out all about my little *gatitos*!

All the kittens liked licking the anchovies, but no one really liked the octopus.

The mummy cat told me that octopus was a bit chewy for growing kittens and that I should try stealing some different meaty things from the buffet.

Miffy told me she preferred chicken to beef, Marble said he quite liked prawns without their shells on.

Midnight asked me to take the bones out of the sea bream, and Smoky told me that if I could get him some really big bits of tuna that would be even better.

Plus Mini Moo asked me to take all the milk out of the milk jugs at breakfast.

So I did!

Well, me and Harrison did.

The trouble with hunting for meat is you have to make sure nobody sees you.

Every chance we got, we nabbed some meat for the kittens.

We got spicy sausage from the tops of Carly's mum and dad's pizza, Spanish ham from my mum's *Olé!* salad, some tuna mayonnaise out of Matty's mum's sandwich, and a whole sardine off Derek's plate when he was talking to my mum.

And no one ever saw us!

Well, not at first they didn't.

Angelo kept the gate unlocked for us every day, so whenever we wanted to visit or feed the kittens, we could.

And so could Jo-Jo.

So for Harrison, me and now Jo-Jo, EVERY DAY of our holiday was GATITO DAY!

We still played with Carly, Cerise, Montague, Matty and Danny in the pool. But we never ever gave away the secret of the kittens. No way José!

No one even got suspicious. Because whenever we wanted to see the kittens we just threw the Frisbee over the fence! So nobody ever knew!

It was brilliant!

I even thought of something to spend my holiday money on that was brilliant too . . .

Kitten food! Real actual proper tins of it that you could buy in the supermarket down by the beach. Mum said kitten food was a silly thing to spend all my holiday money on. She said I should spend my holiday money on postcards or a beach ball or a sunhat.

But after Harrison and me got caught walking out of the evening buffet with a whole salmon, we were banned from stealing any more food from anywhere in the hotel by the hotel manager.

And the pool bar manager.

And our mums.

We couldn't even leave our tables without opening our napkins!

So I JUST HAD to spend ALL my holiday money on proper kitten food. Otherwise the kittens would have died of nothing to eat!

So the next morning after breakfast, Mum took me into the town to look at some real Spanish shops.

Chapter 17

The **trouble with real Spanish shops** is most of them don't sell kitten food at all!

The shops Mum kept taking me to only sold clothes!

Mum said she wanted to find a nice summer dress that she could wear to the tappers bar with Derek on Thursday evening.

Which made me even crosser.

I mean, how could anyone think about buying summer dresses to tap in when five little kittens were starving of something to eat back at the hotel?

Then she started looking for some new shoes!

She'd already put eight pairs in the suitcase; now she was looking for another pair!

It was a good job there was really cold air conditioning in the supermarket, otherwise I would have exploded like a hot-air balloon when I got there.

Mum said that if I didn't chill a bit, she would stick my head in the freezer compartment with the frozen peas.

But Spain doesn't grow peas. It only grows coconuts and lemons, so I knew that wasn't true.

Plus you're not allowed to put

children in freezer cabinets. In any country in the world.

I didn't go near the frozen food bit though, just in case. I had to go all the way round the soap powders and along the cereals to find the kitten food. After we'd paid, my mum asked me if I'd like to go to the beach.

But the **trouble with beaches** is they don't have any kittens on them.

So I said no.

Then she asked me if I'd like to walk down to the harbour to look at the boats.

But the **trouble with boats and harbours** is they don't have any kittens in them either.

So I said no.

Then she asked me if I wanted to go and watch the carnival.

But the trouble with carnivals is they don't have kittens in them either.

So we went back to the hotel instead.

After Mum had put the tins of kitten food in our room, she asked me if I wanted to play ping-pong.

But you know the trouble with

ping-pong tables, don't you?

So Mum gave up after that, and told me she was going to the pool bar to talk to Derek.

Which was BRILLIANT! That meant I could go and feed the kittens with Harrison and Jo-Jo.

I couldn't wait to give the kittens their first taste of actual proper Spanish kitten food out of a tin!

Angelo helped me open the tin and then tip it out onto a saucer for them. And he let me chop it up into little pieces with a fork. When the kittens tried it for the first time, you should have heard the purrs

they made. Marble even GROWLED, it tasted so nice!

Angelo told me I was very kind to buy the little *gatitos* proper *gatito* food.

Then the mummy cat told me in cat-speak that I was the kindest person they had ever met. Even kinder than Angelo! Which made me feel really proud!

Then guess what?

Mini Moo asked me if it would be all right if she called me Mum too!

Then all the kittens said it! They all wanted me to be their second mum!

How brilliant was that?!

The mummy cat said she didn't mind one bit if her kittens called me Mum, because I was so kind and because looking after five babies was really hard work. So any help I could give her would be brilliant.

So I decided to help her even more. Because she asked me to.

Because all the kittens asked me to. All five of them.

Plus the mummy cat, which makes six.

WHICH WASN'T MY FAULT!

Chapter 18

I'm not exactly sure which of my mum's screams was the loudest when she woke up in our hotel bed on Thursday morning.

The scream she did when she opened her eyes and found five kittens on the pillows between us . . .

Or the scream she did when she looked in the bathroom mirror.

Both of them were pretty loud.

Very loud actually.

The **trouble with sleeping with kittens** is (and there is NO WAY I could ever have known this) – kittens have fleas.

Especially kittens who live next to dustbins.

The **trouble with fleas** is . . . er . . . they bite.

They bite your arms, they bite your tummy, they bite your face while you're asleep, and they make you itchy in all the places they've bitten you. Except . . .

. . . the **REALLY BIG TROUBLE with flea bites** is (and there is NO WAY I could EVER, EVER have been meant to know this – I mean, EVEN my mum didn't know this until the hotel doctor came and told her . . .) – the **BIGGEST trouble with flea bites** is . . .

. . . my mum's allergic to them!

I'm not. My flea bites were only small and felt a bit itchy. But my mum is absolutely allergic to flea bites **BIG TIME!**

That's why her face had gone all puffy. And the rest of her body too.

"WHAT HAVE YOU DONE TO ME, DAISY?!" she shouted. "I LOOK LIKE THE ELEPHANT MAN!"

Which wasn't true because she didn't have a trunk or anything.

"WHAT ON EARTH POSSESSED YOU TO PUT FIVE KITTENS IN OUR BED?!"

"I was baby-sitting them," I said. "Their mum wanted a night off,

so I said I would help her out. I had to put them in our bed or they might have got cold."

But my mum didn't believe me.

"COLD!?" she said. "IT'S THIRTY DEGREES OUTSIDE AT NIGHT!! HOW ON EARTH ARE FIVE FURRY KITTENS GOING TO GET COLD IN THIRTY DEGREES OF BAKING-HOT SPANISH NIGHT?!"

So I had to think of another answer.

"I thought they might get lonely," I said.

"LONELY??" she said. "THEY'VE GOT TEN MILLION FLEAS TO KEEP THEM

COMPANY!! THE ONLY COMPANY THOSE KITTENS NEED IS A FLEA COMB, MY GIRL!!!"

Trouble is, then she went back into the bathroom and looked in the mirror again.

"LOOK AT MY FACE NOW!" she said. "IT'S EVEN MORE SWOLLEN!!

"LOOK AT MY EYES!!" she said. "THEY'RE STREAMING! LOOK AT MY CHEEKS!! JUST LOOK AT ME, DAISY!! I'VE GOT A FACE LIKE A BOUNCY CASTLE!!!" she said. Well, shouted, actually.

Trouble is, then she looked at her ankles.

"AND LOOK AT MY ANKLES!" she screamed. "THEY'RE WIDER THAN THE TOPS OF MY LEGS! THIS ISN'T A FLEA ALLERGY – IT'S BUBONIC PLAGUE!"

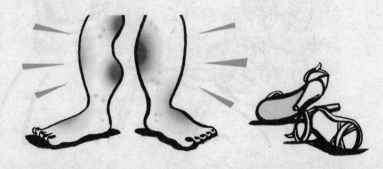

Which wasn't true either. Otherwise her face would have fallen off. Then she went all thoughtful.

"WAIT A MOMENT," she said. "HOW DID YOU GET FIVE KITTENS IN OUR BED IN THE FIRST PLACE? HOW DID YOU EVEN GET THEM INTO THE ROOM?"

So I told her.

"Harrison helped me lift them up through the window," I said.

"THROUGH THE WINDOW?" she puffed. "HARRISON IS FOUR FOOT TALL, DAISY! OUR WINDOW IS TWENTY FEET ABOVE GROUND LEVEL!"

So then I had to tell her a bit more.

"We put the kittens in my rucksack and then I pulled the rucksack up to our window on a bit of string," I said.

"A BIT OF STRING?" huffed my mum. "WHAT BIT OF STRING?" she puffed.

"I found it by the dustbins," I said.

"RUCKSACKS! WINDOWS! KITTENS! BITS OF STRING!" she said. "AND WHERE WAS I WHEN ALL THESE MILITARY MANOEUVRES WERE GOING ON?"

"You were by the front door, talking to Derek," I said.

"OH MY GOD!" she said, going super puffy now. **"I CAN'T GO TO DINNER WITH DEREK LOOKING LIKE THIS!**

I CAN'T EVEN LEAVE THE HOTEL ROOM LOOKING LIKE THIS! WHAT HAVE YOU DONE TO ME, DAISY?!"

"It's not my fault the kittens have got fleas!" I said.

"NO, BUT IT'S YOUR FAULT THE

KITTENS ENDED UP IN OUR BED!!" she said. "ARE YOU MAD, DAISY? HAS THE SPANISH SUN SHRIVELLED UP YOUR BRAINS?!"

The **trouble with talking to mums with huffy puffy faces** is they don't really listen. They just get crosser and crosser.

Especially if then you ask them if you can take five kittens home with you.

Very especially if you do that.

"NO, DAISY, YOU ARE NOT TAKING FIVE KITTENS HOME WITH YOU!" she said. "IN FACT, I'LL TELL YOU WHERE YOU CAN TAKE THOSE KITTENS . . . YOU CAN TAKE THEM RIGHT BACK TO THE FILTHY DUSTBINS WHERE YOU FOUND THEM! IN FACT, YOU CAN PUT THEM IN THE DUSTBIN FOR ALL I CARE!"

So I did.

Not *in. Beside.*

I took them all the way back to the dustbins and put them back next to their number one mum.

I guess that's where they belonged.

Chapter 19

When I told Angelo that my mum had fleas and her face had gone all puffy, he said it might be a good idea if I stayed out of her way for a little while. He said maybe it would be better if I stayed in the pool until her face went down a bit.

But the **trouble with face puff** is it doesn't go down for ages.

Especially when it's flea face puff.

So I decided I'd better go and tell Derek.

"YOU TOLD DEREK WHAT?!" my mum huffed and puffed at me when I finally went back to our room.

"I told him you had fleas," I said.

"YOU TOLD DEREK **I HAD FLEAS**!!!!" she said. "OH MY

WORD . . . THIS JUST GOES FROM BAD TO WORSE!"

"Well, you have, haven't you?" I said. "The doctor said you have."

"THE DOCTOR SAID I HAVE A FLEA ALLERGY, DAISY! HE DIDN'T SAY I HAD FLEAS!!" she said.

"I thought he did," I said.

"OH MY GOD . . . AND HOW MANY OTHER PEOPLE HAVE YOU TOLD THAT I HAVE FLEAS?" asked my mum.

"Only Angelo," I said.

"And Danny and Harrison and Jo-Jo and Carly and Montague and Cerise.

"And Cerise's mum."

The **trouble with telling your mum you've told everyone she has fleas** is even her ears will start to go puffy after that.

And her eyes will go all bulgy.

"BRILLIANT!" she said. (But I don't think she meant it.)

"BRILLIANT BRILLIANT BRILLIANT!! I KNOW, DAISY . . . WHY DON'T WE PUT UP A BIG NOTICE IN THE HOTEL LOBBY AND TELL THE WHOLE WORLD

THAT YOUR MUM HAS FLEAS?"

(But I don't think she meant that either.)

"BEDTIME FOR YOU, MY GIRL AND ROOM SERVICE FOR ME . . . AND TONIGHT, DAISY, YOU CAN SLEEP ON THE SOFA!"

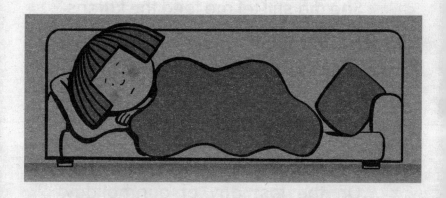

Trouble was, she definitely DID mean that.

Mum didn't come out of our hotel room again after that. Apart from when we had to take our suitcases to the coach on Saturday.

She kept the curtains drawn in our room all day Friday, while I played in the pool with my friends.

She did still let me feed the kittens, but only because she said there was no way we were carrying six tins of cat food home on the plane. And there was no way we were taking five kittens home with us on the plane!

On the last day of our holiday, when I went to say goodbye to the kittens, I thought I was going to cry.

But I didn't.

Angelo made me feel better. He said that Spanish *gatitos* get very shivery in English weather and that the best place for them was here in the warm Spanish sunshine beside the dustbins next to their other mum.

Then he promised me that he would help look after them as well as I had, until I came back to the hotel with my mum, perhaps next year.

When we went home, my mum's ankles were so fat, she had to be pushed in a wheelchair all the way through the airport and lifted up the stairs of the plane.

She wasn't very happy. She said she had wanted to come back from Spain looking like a bronzed beauty but had ended up looking like an over-boiled dumpling.

I told her I was really sorry about the fleas, and if we came back next

year, I would triple promise not to let the kittens sleep with us in the same bed.

But I think her ears were so puffed up she couldn't hear.

Never mind. At least I had a brilliant time!

I found the cutest little *gatitos* in the world!

I learned how to do Spanish cat-speak.

I learned how to play Zombie Mermaids and Zombie Frisbees!

I swapped addresses with Harrison and Jo-Jo before I left so now I can write letters to them whenever I want.

I even learned how to open real kitten-food tins with a tin opener!

But do you know what makes me smile about my holiday more

than anything?

Those clever little *gatitos*, getting me out of going to dinner with that horrible Derek!

Wink, wink!

DAISY'S
TROUBLE
INDEX

The trouble with . . .

To Oliver Edward Andrews

DAISY

and the TROUBLE with

COCONUTS

by Kes Gray

RED FOX

CHAPTER 1

The **trouble with coconuts** is they are the worst type of nuts in the whole wide world.

If I was a monkey living in a jungle that was totally made up of coconut trees, and one of the coconuts on one of the trees asked me to be their friend, then there is absolutely no way that I would say yes. I'd rather be friends with Jack Beechwhistle, who's the worst boy on earth, than be friends with a coconut.

If you ask me, coconuts shouldn't be allowed in a funfair. If you double ask me, they shouldn't even be allowed to grow. Coconuts are too big. Coconuts are too hairy. Plus, if you try to win one, they just get you into trouble.

WHICH ISN'T MY FAULT!

CHAPTER 2

I was really excited when I heard that the funfair was coming to town. Gabby was the first person at school to tell me. Nishta Bagwhat was second. Daniel McNicholl was third.

Fiona Tucker was fourth, I think. Or it might have been Colin Kettle, I'm not sure. So I'll call it a draw.

Everyone in the playground was really excited about the funfair. Trouble is, everyone was still really excited when we went into class too. Being excited about funfairs in class is against school rules. Because it makes you forget your times tables. And it makes you fidget.

The **trouble with fidgeting** is it makes your chair squeak.

The **trouble with chairs squeaking** is it makes your teacher look right at you. Which is a bit of a problem if you've just said six sevens are 93.

If you've just told your teacher that six sevens are 93, you really want her to ask someone else the next sum.

Trouble is, when Mrs Peters heard my chair squeak again, she asked me two sums in a row. Which is probably against the law. But there was no one around to stop her.

The **trouble with nine times eight** is it's an even harder sum to do than six times seven. Especially if there's a funfair coming to town.

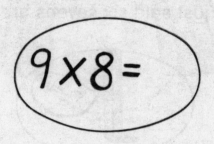

If there's a funfair coming to town, all sums turn into really hard sums because your brain can't stop thinking about more important things.

Like funfairs.

The **trouble with thinking about funfairs during mental arithmetic** is the nines sound a bit like fives and the eights get muddled up with fours.

Which is why I said that the answer to nine times eight was 20.

Which isn't the right answer either.

When Mrs Peters said it wasn't even close, everyone in my class started looking at me. Which made me go all hot.

The **trouble with going all hot in class** is it makes your brain shrink. Which means it's even harder to do sums in your head.

Luckily for me, Jack Beechwhistle fell off his chair just before I was going to change my mind to 76. Which was a good job really. Because 76 wasn't the right answer either.

Thank goodness Jack *did* fall off his chair, because everyone was

looking at him now, instead of me.
Including Mrs Peters.

Except no one could see him.
Because he hadn't got back up off
the floor.

When Fiona Tucker looked down

by her feet and told us that Jack was dead on the floor, Mrs Peters forgot about nine times eight altogether. She ran to the back of the class where Fiona and Jack sit and looked under the desk to see if it was true.

But it wasn't. Jack Beechwhistle wasn't even slightly dead. He was just pretending.

That's the **trouble with Jack Beechwhistle**. He is soooooooooooo badly behaved.

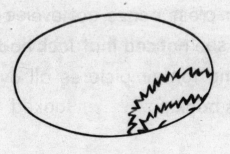

The **trouble with pretending you're dead in class** is Mrs Peters doesn't think it's a very funny thing to do.

Everyone else in class thought it was funny, but Mrs Peters is a teacher. Which means she's had her funny bones taken out and replaced with cross bones.

Her cross bones got even crosser when she noticed that Jack had been drawing funfair pictures all over his maths book.

Then she got even crosser than crosser when she noticed that Fiona Tucker had been drawing funfair pictures too.

It wasn't just Jack and Fiona either.

Nishta had drawn a big wheel on the back of her hand, Harry Bayliss had done a candyfloss

tattoo on his arm and David Alexander had drawn a rifle

range with exploding ducks right across the top of his school bag.

No wonder no one could get their sums right.

Luckily I'd never been to a funfair before, so I didn't know what kind of pictures to draw. But I still got told off for squeaking.

Mrs Peters told us that fidgeting and drawing funfair pictures in mental arithmetic was completely unacceptable behaviour. She said that if Pythagoras had spent all his time fidgeting and drawing candyfloss tattoos on his arms, then mathematics would still be in the Dark Ages.

She said that from now on we must

start concentrating on the important things in life. Then she said we had to stay in at break time to catch up on our sums. Plus we got banned from even thinking about funfairs for the rest of the day.

But I still did. Only in secret and without fidgeting!

CHAPTER 3

The **trouble with funfair posters** is when a funfair comes to town, they stick them everywhere!

When me and Mum went into town after school, I saw funfair posters stuck on the fence down by the roundabout. There were funfair posters stuck on the window of an empty shop in the high street. There were even bits of a funfair poster stuck on the back of a lorry parked outside the baker's.

It was so exciting!

It got even more exciting when Mum told me that Nanny and Grampy had phoned while I was at school and offered to take me to the funfair on Saturday afternoon! I didn't even know that my nanny and grampy liked funfairs! I thought they were far too old to like fun things.

Mum said that just because people are over the age of sixty it doesn't mean they should give up the will to live. She said that, for a lot of people, retirement is the most enjoyable time of life. She said that when you're Nanny and Grampy's age you can do anything you want, any time you want to.

Which is a good job really, because Mum would never have taken me to a funfair. Because Mum doesn't like funfairs at all.

Whenever the funfair has come to town before, my mum has always pulled a grumpy face. As far as she is concerned, funfairs are a complete waste of money. Plus she says the games at a funfair are too expensive and the rides spin you round so much they make you sick.

Sometimes I think my mum should have been a teacher.

Luckily for me, Mum wasn't invited. I reckon Nanny and Grampy had probably taken Mum to a funfair when she was a little girl and had decided never to do it again. Funfairs are no fun at all if you take the wrong sort of children.

Luckily for Nanny and Grampy, I was exactly the right sort of child to take to a funfair. I didn't mind if the rides were too expensive because Nanny and Grampy would be paying! I didn't even mind if the rides made me feel sick, because at least I'd be having brilliant fun at the same time! Plus I was absolutely sure I wasn't going to be sick anyway.

When I spoke to Grampy on the phone on Friday, he sounded even more excited about the funfair than me! He asked me if I'd ever been in a bumper car, and I said I hadn't. He asked me if I'd ever been down a helter-skelter, and I said I hadn't. He asked me if I'd ever been on a waltzer, and I said I hadn't. He asked me if I'd ever eaten a toffee apple, and I said I had.

But I hadn't. Only I said I had because it was getting a bit embarrassing. And anyway, I HAD eaten an apple before. And I HAD eaten a toffee before. Only not at the same time. Which is almost the same thing.

Kind of.

Anyway, Grampy said that there were two things that we absolutely *must* do while we were at the funfair on Saturday.

Number 1: We *must* win a goldfish!

Number 2: We *must* win a coconut!

I'd never won a goldfish or a coconut before, so you can imagine how excited I was now!!

When Nanny came on the phone, she said that they would pick me up in the car at twelve o'clock on Saturday and would bring me back at four.

Which, if you're any good at mental arithmetic, adds up to . . .

. . . **FOUR** FABULOUS FUN-FILLED HOURS!

Maybe staying in at break time *did* help me with my sums after all!

CHAPTER 4

The **trouble with normal breakfasts** is they can be a bit boring.

So when I woke up on Saturday I decided that instead of having a normal breakfast, I would have a special funfair one. Funfair breakfasts are much more fun. In fact they're so much fun, you don't even need to put sugar on them!

To have a funfair breakfast, all you need is two Weetabixes and some Honey Nut Loops. Oh, and a biggish carton of milk with quite a lottish amount of milk in.

Here are my instructions on how to make Daisy's Special Funfair Breakfast:

First of all, take the first Weetabix and lay it flat on the bottom of your bowl.

Then wedge the second Weetabix up against it like a slide. (The first Weetabix helps the second Weetabix stay in position.)

Next, cover the flat Weetabix with milk. Not too much – just enough to make the milk look like a swamp.

Then, take a Honey Nut Loop in your fingers, place it at the top of the slide, count down from three to one, let go of the Honey Nut Loop and let it roll down the slide into the swamp!

As soon as the loop touches the side of your bowl, you can grab it out with your fingers and eat it!

How much fun is that?!

The more Honey Nut Loops you roll down the slide, the more you get to eat!! It's simple! Plus, once you've run out of Honey Nut Loops you can eat the slide while it's still crunchy and the mushy bottom of the swamp afterwards!!

Mum said I could have funfair breakfasts every day if it meant I was going to eat that much breakfast for breakfast.

I said I would if I could go to a funfair every day too.

But she said I couldn't.

So I said I probably wouldn't.

CHAPTER 5

It was a really hot day on Saturday, so getting dressed after breakfast took hardly any time at all. I was sure the funfair would be full of bright colours

so I decided to wear my brand-new orange shorts plus my brightest coloured T-shirt and socks.

Mum said I looked a bit clashy, but I didn't care. I think orange, purple and green go really well together.

Once I was dressed, I went into the lounge to practise my screaming. Gabby had told me that some of the rides at a funfair are so good, you can't stop screaming from the moment you get on!

The **trouble with practising screaming** is I'm too good at it.

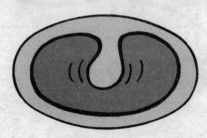

Mum said that if I wanted to practise my screaming I should go and do it outside in the garden.

But after about five screams our neighbour Mrs Pike told me that I should practise in the shed.

With the door shut.

So I did.

Except Tiptoes was asleep in the wheelbarrow.

The **trouble with screaming when Tiptoes is asleep in the wheelbarrow** is it doesn't just wake him up, it makes him go totally loopy.

I mean, one minute he was curled up in the wheelbarrow; the next minute he was halfway up the wall, then the other wall and then almost across the ceiling!

I wouldn't have screamed if I'd known he was there, but it was so dark in the shed there was no way I could see a cat curled up in the shadows.

That's the **trouble with cats**. If they wore fluorescent pyjamas when they went to sleep, they'd be much easier to see.

By the time I'd opened the shed door to let Tiptoes out, he'd knocked over the flower pots, the rake, the watering can, the spade, the fork, plus all the seed packets that were on the highest-up shelf.

And guess who had to pick them all up? It wasn't Tiptoes. It was me!

If you ask me, if a cat wants to curl up and go to sleep in a wheelbarrow he should get his own shed to sleep in. And his own wheelbarrow.

Or at least wear glow-in-the-dark pyjamas.

Or learn to snore loudly.

It was only when I was stretching

up high to put the seed packets back that I suddenly forgave Tiptoes for everything. Because all of my really high up stretching and stretching suddenly reminded me of something really important that Dylan had told me at school!

If you're going to go to a funfair . . .

. . . you need to wear your highest shoes!

CHAPTER 6

Dylan is the coolest boy I know. He's two years older than me, which means he's really experienced. Plus he lives two doors away from me in a house with a three-chime doorbell. AND he's got a pet snake  called Shooter. How cool is that?

At first, when Dylan told me that I needed to wear my highest shoes to the funfair on Saturday, I thought he was joking. But Dylan is far too cool to do jokes. Sometimes Dylan is too cool to even smile.

According to Dylan, some of the rides at a funfair are so dangerous and so death-defying, you have to be over 140 centimetres to go on them! Trouble is, I'm only 134 centimetres tall.

The **trouble with being 134 centimetres tall** is that if you want to go on all the rides, you need to find an extra six centimetres from somewhere.

Trouble is, I didn't really know where to look.

When I asked my mum on Saturday morning what I needed to eat if I wanted to grow six centimetres in two hours, she wasn't very helpful at all.

"You could try eating some giraffe burgers," she laughed.

I don't know why she was laughing because it wasn't a very funny thing to say at all. Plus I couldn't try eating giraffe burgers because we don't have any giraffe burgers in our freezer.

We don't even have any cow burgers in our freezer any more, because my new super-health-conscious mum has suddenly decided that things that taste really nice like burgers aren't very good for me.

Or chicken nuggets.

According to my mum, it's time I started putting some healthier things inside me. Like fish without breadcrumbs and broccoli without tomato sauce.

Mum watches far too much telly, if you ask me. Plus she's useless at helping to find extra centimetres.

The **trouble with putting on your mum's high heels** is if she sees you, she'll make you take them straight off.

The **trouble with wearing two pairs of shoes at once** is the first pair keep falling off.

The **trouble with sellotaping books to the bottom of your shoes** is the sellotape unsticks after about six steps, plus if the books belong to your mum, she gets a bit cross.

Especially if she hasn't read them yet.

Which means you STILL need to find another six centimetres from somewhere.

In the end my mum convinced me I didn't need to find six centimetres from anywhere. She said I wasn't going to a theme park where the rides are massive, I was going to a travelling funfair where the rides would be much smaller and not that death-defying at all.

Which was a bit disappointing really, because I wanted all the rides at the funfair to be as deathly death-defying as possible.

Mum said if I wanted to do something deathly death-defying, then I should try tidying my bedroom. Which wasn't funny either.

Then she said that there would be more than enough rides for me to go on at the funfair, more than enough rides for Nanny and Grampy to waste their money on, and more than enough rides to make me feel sick.

Which meant that 134 centimetres would be ample.

And actually, she was right.

For once.

She isn't usually right about anything. She's usually always wrong.

But I still put three pairs of socks on just in case!

CHAPTER 7

When Nanny and Grampy arrived outside our house in their car, I nearly screamed I was so excited!

"Are you ready to win a goldfish, Daisy?" shouted Grampy as he opened the door of his car.

"I sure am!" I shouted back.

"Are you ready to win a coconut?" he shouted as he opened the garden gate for Nanny.

"You bet!" I shouted back.

If I could have, I would have run straight out of the front door, raced down the garden path and jumped straight into their car through the sunroof, I was so excited!

Trouble is, Mum made me put some sun cream on first.

The **trouble with putting on sun cream** is it takes ages. Especially if it's a hot day, because more of your burny bits are on show.

Which meant Nanny and Grampy had to come into our house and wait for me.

Which meant Mum had a chance to talk to them about some really boring stuff like:

"Don't let Daisy get over over-excited," and "Don't let Daisy go on rides that will make her sick."

Honestly, sometimes I wonder if Mum was ever an actual child herself.

If she was, I bet she never got sunburned.

Mum made me put so much sun cream on, it was twenty past twelve before we even left the house!

Grampy said I looked like a polar bear when I got in the car.

That's the **trouble with sun cream for children**. Children don't want to put it on in the first place, plus when you're made to, it's all white and smeary.

The **trouble with short-sleeved T-shirts** is the sleeves are too short to wipe your face on.

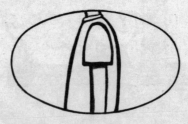

The **trouble with wiping your face on your arms** is if your arms are white and smeary too, then the white from your face will smear onto your arms and the white from your arms will smear onto your face.

Which means that, after loads of wiping, you still look like a polar bear!

I mean, why can't sun cream for children be invisible? Why does it have to make them look like polar bears?

I mean, grown-up sun cream isn't thick and white and smeary, is it? Sun cream for grown-ups is invisible. Which means it just makes grown-ups look like grown-ups. Only slimier.

That's definitely something I'm going to invent when I'm older. Invisible non-smeary sun cream for children.

And extra-thick extra-white extra-smeary sun cream for grown-ups. So *they* can look like polar bears instead. Which will serve them right.

Luckily Nanny had some tissues in her handbag. Otherwise I don't know what I'd have done.

Nanny had mints in her handbag too! Which made me feel even better.

The **trouble with mints** is they're really hard to suck. Especially when you're driving to a funfair.

The **trouble with driving to a funfair** is it makes your teeth get excited.

The **trouble with excited teeth** is it's almost impossible to stop them from biting. Which is a bit of a problem really if your grampy suddenly says, "I know. Let's all play a game! Let's see who can suck a mint for the longest without crunching!"

At first I thought it was a really good idea for a game to play in the car. In fact, at first I did some really good sucks.

Then I saw the funfair poster down by the roundabout.

The **trouble with seeing a funfair poster** is your gums get excited too.

Then I counted three more funfair posters in the high street.

Which meant my tongue got excited.

Then I saw someone carrying a balloon that I was absolutely sure must have come from the funfair.

Which made my taste buds get excited.

And then, as we got nearer and nearer to the park, I actually heard actual funfair sounds coming through the actual sunroof of our actual car!

When I wound down my window, the sounds got even louder.

Which meant my everything buds got excited.

By the time we got to the car park and I got to actually *see* the funfair with my own eyes, even my dribble was excited!!!!!!!!!!

Which meant I had to crunch.

Which meant I lost the game.

Plus I bit my tongue.

Which hurt a bit. But it was OK.

Because for the first time ever in my life, it was

FUNFAIR, HERE I COME!

CHAPTER 8

The **trouble with seeing an actual funfair right in front of you** is you don't know where to look first!!!

It was so bright and colourful and noisy and busy! There were coloured lights and loud screaming sounds, there were big stripy tents held up by big thick ropes.

Plus there were people and children everywhere. It was as though everyone in the whole wide world had come to have fun at the funfair. Except my mum.

And guess what?

You didn't even have to pay to get in! All we had to do was park our car in the field, walk across the grass and go straight inside!

I didn't even have to be measured to see how high I was!

It was so brilliant! And so confusing! My left leg wanted to go left, my right leg wanted to go right, and my head – well, my head just wanted to go everywhere.

Before I'd had time to even think about goldfish or coconuts, I ran straight over to a stall with a green and yellow stripy roof and a big red sign with gold letters that said TOMBOLA!

Tombola is a really exciting funfair game. Once you have paid a lady some money you get to pick three chopped-up straws out of a bucket of sawdust. All the straws have rolled-up raffle tickets inside them, and if one of the raffle tickets has a number that ends in zero, you win a prize!

I was really good at pulling the rolled-up raffle tickets out of my straws, and even better at getting them to uncurl.

Trouble is, the raffle tickets I picked out of the bucket ended in 3, 6 and 9.

Which means I didn't win a prize. But it was OK, because there were loads of other stalls with flashing lights and stripy roofs to choose from.

The next game I tried was called hook-a-duck.

The **trouble with hook-a-duck** is you really need to be an expert fisherman to be good at it. Which is a shame for other children, because they haven't been taught to fish by my uncle Clive. Luckily I have.

Hook-a-duck is one of the most skilful funfair games you can ever play. Once you have paid a man some money, he gives you a stick with a string and a magnet dangling from it. That's your hook-a-duck fishing rod.

But then it gets even harder!

Not only have you got to learn how to dangle the string and the magnet from the end of your rod; you have to lean over a great big tank full of actual water at the same time!

And then it gets even harder!

Because the tank of water is where all the ducks are floating!!!

(Not actual ducks. Yellow plastic ones. With magnets on their backs.)

And then it gets even harder!

Because what you have to do then is use your hook-a-duck fishing rod to try and hook a duck out of the water!

The **trouble with a hook-a-duck duck** is it can only get hooked out if you can get the magnet at the end of your string to stick to the magnet on its back!

Which means you need to be a total fishing expert.

Which I am. So I did! In about seven seconds flat!

When I lifted my hook-a-duck duck out of the water I thought I was going to be able to keep it as a prize. But the hook-a-duck man turned my h o o k - a - d u c k duck upside down and showed me a black cross that had been felt-tipped onto its tummy.

A black cross means you can't keep the duck. And you haven't won a prize either. Which was a bit of a shame, but it didn't really matter

because I had already seen the next game I wanted to play!

It was in a tent about ten kangaroo jumps away and it was a game I'd always, always wanted to play . . . actual DARTS!

To play actual darts you have to pay a lady some money and then she gives you three actual darts! The actual darts she gave me looked just like the ones you see on telly, only a bit fatter, with yellow plastic bits on the end. At first I thought the sharp bits might have been dipped in poison, but Nanny said you aren't allowed to have poison darts at a funfair.

The **trouble with actual darts** is it's a lot harder to play than it looks. Especially if you're only 134 centimetres tall.

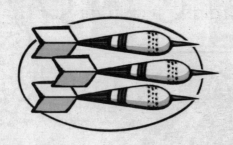

To win a prize at actual darts you have to throw all three darts at the dartboard and score less than 21. Which sounds easy, but is actually really hard.

When I went up to throw my first dart, I could hardly see the dartboard, which meant when I let go of the dart it kind of didn't go in the dartboard at all. It went in the lady's shoulder.

Luckily it didn't have poison on it and it didn't stick in very far. Otherwise

she wouldn't have let me have that go again. But she probably still would have got me a box to stand on.

When you're playing actual darts and you've got a box to stand on, the dartboard is much easier to see. Trouble is, it doesn't make it much easier to hit.

The **trouble with fat darts with yellow bits** is that when you throw them they never go straight.

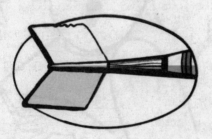

Plus, even when they hit the dartboard, they don't stick in.

My first dart nearly hit the dartboard. My second dart nearly hit the dartboard. My third dart DEFINITELY hit the dartboard, but it still ended up on the ground.

Which, if you add up all the scores, is zero. Which is definitely less than 21.

When I asked the lady for my prize, she told me that if the dart doesn't stick in the dartboard it counts as 1000. Which meant I'd scored 3000. Which is slightly more than 21.

When I asked if I could have

another go, Nanny and Grampy said we should probably move on. So did the lady.

Which was a good idea actually, because now I was about to go on my first ride!

CHAPTER 9

When I saw the bumper cars, I nearly wet myself! Bumper cars are totally the best! Not only has the bumper-car track got hundreds of flashing lights and really loud music, it's got cars you can actually drive!

And crash!

On purpose!!!!!!

Grampy said he loved going on bumper cars when he was a boy and he would come in my bumper car with me.

I said I definitely, definitely wanted

to be the driver!

Trouble is, you can't just get in and drive a bumper car straight away. You have to wait around the edge until all the people in the cars finish their go first.

When the hooter went and the bumper cars started to slow down, I had already worked out which one I wanted to drive. It was a bright shiny red one with a big grey rubber bumping bit round it. Plus it had my lucky number 8 on both sides!

As soon as the cars came to a proper stop I raced straight across to car number 8 and waited for the boy inside it to get out. Trouble is, he was a bit slow undoing his seat belt.

The **trouble with boys who are slow at undoing seat belts** is it makes you really impatient with them.

The **trouble with trying to undo their seat belt for them** is they don't really like it. Especially if they're about fifteen.

When I grabbed the boy's seat-belt buckle, he got really huffy and pushed my hand away. I think he was nearly going to say something not very nice to me, but then he saw that Grampy wanted to get into the bumper car with me, so he didn't say anything at all.

But even if he had I wouldn't have cared, because now I was sitting behind the wheel of my very own bumper car!

When I squeezed my fingers around my bumper car steering wheel, I got racing car tingles right through my body.

When Grampy fastened my seat belt, I felt like a grand-prix driver off the telly!

At first we started off quite slowly, but after about ten seconds I was driving our bumper car at full speed!

If I turned the steering wheel to the left, we went to the left! If I turned the wheel to the right, we went to the right. And if a car stopped in front of me, I could press my speed pedal as hard as I could and crash right into the back of them! Without saying sorry!

It was bumptastic!!!

Grampy asked me if I'd been taking driving lessons from my mum.

Then he told me to wave to Nanny.

The **trouble with waving to Nanny** is if you're driving a bumper car at the same time, you might miss someone you should be crashing into.

Luckily Grampy grabbed the steering wheel and made sure we bumped straight into car number 22!

And then car number 7, car number 12 and car number 9!

Grampy said we should try and crash into every single car before the hooter went! Trouble is, then the bumper-car man jumped onto the back of our car and told us we weren't allowed to bump.

Apparently we weren't in a bumper car, we were in a dodgem

car. Which meant bumping wasn't allowed. We had to dodge instead.

The **trouble with dodging cars instead of bumping them** is it's still really good fun but crashing into people is much better.

Grampy said it was health and safety gone mad, so we kept on doing it and doing it and doing it! Until I hit my chin on the steering wheel.

329

Which wasn't my fault. It was car number 14's fault.

The **trouble with car number 14** is I don't think the driver can have heard the hooter.

After the hooter goes you're not meant to bump anyone any more.

So when car number 14 suddenly crashed into me from behind, I couldn't stop myself from crashing forward and hitting my chin. Because I wasn't expecting to be bumped.

Luckily it wasn't my nose, because that really would have hurt! It still made me feel a little bit dizzy though.

Grampy said that if you bump someone in a dodgem car, it makes them want to bump you back. Even after the hooter has hooted.

Grampy undid my seat belt, had a good look at my chin, gave it a rub and said that these things happen, especially when there are maniac drivers around.

Which makes you think, doesn't it?

Why, oh, why don't bumper cars have airbags?

CHAPTER 10

The **trouble with being in a car accident** is it makes you need a fizzy drink.

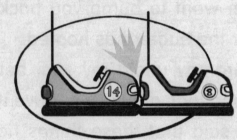

The **trouble with fizzy drinks** is there are so many different ones to choose from.

And non-fizzy ones! Especially at a funfair!

By the time I got to the fizzy drinks stall, I'd forgotten all about the bump on my chin. Fizzy drinks stalls give children much more important things to think about. Like cola, or cherryade, or lemonade or orangeade or, even better . . . wait for it . . .

. . . SLUSH PUPPIES!

When I saw that the fizzy drinks stall did slush puppies, I really did scream! Slush puppies are my favouritest drink that I'm not allowed to have. They're like milkshakes except they take all the milk out and put icy slush in instead. My mum never lets me have slush puppies because she says they're full of colourings and artificial flavourings and other things that sound really nice.

But guess what? My mum wasn't with us!

There are four flavours of slush puppy that you can choose from at a funfair. Green, red, orange and bright blue. Nanny and Grampy said I could have any flavour I wanted.

So after they had given the lady some money, I asked for red.

Mixed with bright blue.

Which makes bright purple if you

mix it up with a straw.

Bright purple slush puppies are the best! You should try one!

After I'd finished my slush puppy, Nanny said we should think about getting something to eat. Which was a brilliant idea, because my slush puppy had made me feel really hungry.

The **trouble with funfair hotdogs and burgers** is it's really hard to choose which one is nicest. Especially when the burgers are extra large and the sausages are extra long and bendy.

So Nanny said I could have one of each! So I did!

Without onions though.

The **trouble with funfair onions** is they look a bit burned and squishy.

Plus if you don't have any, it leaves much more room for tomato sauce.

After I'd eaten my hotdog and burger I thought I was absolutely full. But then I suddenly realized I wasn't! Because guess what I saw next?

CANDYFLOSS!

The **trouble with candyfloss** is when you see somewhere that makes it, it makes you do two things:

1. Scream.

2. Scream again!!

Have you ever seen how candy-floss is made? It's incredible! You just give a man some money and then he takes an empty stick and waves it round and round like a magic wand

inside this special metal machine where all the candyfloss is being fluffed up. The more waving he does, the more the candyfloss fluffs up onto your stick!

Nanny and Grampy asked the candyfloss man for an extra-large one, which meant by the time he had stopped fluffing, the candyfloss on my stick was huge!

In fact, it was bigger than my face!

Luckily I'm quite strong so I could hold it in one hand.

When I took my first bite of candyfloss, I couldn't believe it. It was like eating a pink sugary cloud! It tasted really sweet and really good for me, except every time I tried to chew it, it just melted away in my mouth! Big chews, little chews, tiny nibbles, weeny sucks – whichever way I tried to eat it, it just kept disappearing in my mouth.

Even if I just touched it with my tongue, it melted away!

After about twenty bites, Nanny showed me how to pull bits off with my fingers. If you pull candyfloss off with your fingers, it doesn't melt

341

away at all. Until you put it in your mouth.

Then Nanny showed me how to use my candyfloss to pretend I had a moustache like Grampy's!

Only mine was a moustache I could eat!

"I've got a good idea!" I said. "I'll make a long candyfloss beard as well and pretend I'm Father Christmas!"

Trouble is, I didn't have enough candyfloss left on my stick by

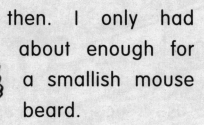

then. I only had about enough for a smallish mouse beard.

Which was OK, because now we were going on the waltzer!

CHAPTER 11

The **trouble with waltzers** is everybody wants to go on them. Which means we had to queue up in a line for about five minutes before we could get on.

Grampy said the queue would give my slush puppy and hotdog and burger and tomato sauce and candyfloss a chance to go down. But it also gave me a chance to say hello to Sanjay Lapore!

At first I didn't even realize that Sanjay and his mum and dad were standing in the queue behind us! I was far too busy watching the waltzer, trying to work out which carriage would be the fastest one for us to get into.

Sanjay asked me if I'd seen any friends from school. He said loads of people from school were at the funfair too – he had seen Liam Chaldecott, Liberty Pearce, Barry Morely, Vicky Carrow, Paula Potts and even Mrs Peters!

Can you believe it?! Mrs Peters!!!!
I never thought she would like funfairs too!

Sanjay told me that, so far, he'd been on the merry-go-round and the octopus. Plus he'd nearly won a teddy on the claw of destiny.

When I asked him what a claw of destiny was, he said it was a really exciting game in a glass box where you have to try and pick up a teddy by steering and dropping down a shiny metal claw.

Sanjay's dad is a crane driver so Sanjay

knew he would be really good at the claw of destiny. Trouble is, the claw dropped into the teddies before it was supposed to and then it closed up before it was supposed to as well. Which meant that Sanjay touched a teddy but didn't actually pick it up. But he was really close!

When I asked him what an octopus did, he said it was a really scary giant ride with eight legs that spins you round and round in the air! Plus it waves you up and down so much it nearly throws you out of the fairground!

When I asked him if it made him

scream, he said he screamed so loud, his ears nearly fell off!

When we got to the front of the queue for the waltzer, Nanny asked Sanjay's mum and dad if they wanted to get in our carriage with us. Waltzer carriages are easily big enough to fit six people in, so now it was going to be six times as much fun!

Waltzers are really death-defying. In fact they are so death-defying you don't get normal seat belts to save you, you get safety bars made out of actual metal!

Which is a good job really because waltzers are out of control!! Not only do they make you go faster than a rocket, they move you up and down as well!

After about twenty-seven seconds, we were all screaming so much we didn't even realize there was a steering wheel we could turn in the middle of our carriage. But when we noticed someone else doing it, we worked out how to make our carriage spin round too!

At first, Sanjay and me took turns with the wheel, but then our face muscles started to hurt so much from all our laughing and screaming that we had to stop. Which was OK,

because then Sanjay's dad did the wheel-turning instead.

You should have seen Nanny and Grampy's faces as we got spinnier and spinnier! Grampy's wrinkles went right over to one side of his face! And Nanny screamed so much, her false teeth nearly came out of her mouth!

I think Nanny and Grampy were really relieved when the waltzer started to slow down. Sanjay and me weren't. We wanted to stay on and have another go!

But we weren't allowed to.

Which was OK, because as the safety bars in our waltzer unlocked,

I saw another funfair game that I absolutely totally wanted to go on.

It was a Wild West game called rootin' tootin' shoot 'em. And guess what? It was a game with actual guns!

CHAPTER 12

The **trouble with actual guns** is Sanjay's mum and dad don't think children should be allowed to play with them.

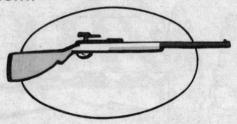

So we had to say goodbye to Sanjay and his mum and dad after that. Which was OK, because six people aren't allowed to hold a rootin' tootin' cowboy rifle at the same time.

Rootin' tootin' shoot 'em is one of the most dangerous things you can do at a funfair, because – and you're never going to believe this – it's a game with real actual rifles, loaded with real actual corks!

Once Grampy had paid a man in a cowboy hat some money, I was given five actual corks to shoot, all of my very own!!! Plus I was allowed to stand up on a box so I could reach my gun!

That's when I got to see what Grampy and me had to aim at. That's when I realized what a good shot I was going to have to be.

Because our targets weren't Indians or buffaloes.

They were boxes of dolly mixtures.

The **trouble with dolly mixtures** is they're a lot smaller than Indians and buffaloes. Which makes them a lot harder to aim at. And hit.

Grampy said to pretend I was Jesse James, but I don't think pop stars know anything about shooting dolly mixtures.

So I just decided to aim as best I could.

The **trouble with rootin' tootin' rifles** is they are quite heavy, which makes them hard to lift.

The **trouble with rootin' tootin' corks** is they don't know how to aim properly.

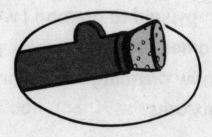

EVERY time the man in the cowboy hat loaded a cork for me, it came out of my rifle the wrong way when I shot it.

If I aimed a cork at the middle of the dolly mixtures, it went *over* the dolly mixtures.

If I aimed my cork over the dolly mixtures, it went *under* the dolly mixtures.

If I pointed my cork to the left, it went to the right.

And if I pointed my cork to the right, it went to the left!

Even Grampy couldn't hit a box of dolly mixtures. And he had five

corks too! Plus he was a soldier in
the war! At least I think he was.

On my last cork, I didn't even aim
at the dolly mixtures. I just pointed it
in the air and pulled the trigger.

And guess what?

I HIT THE DOLLY MIXTURES! I knocked an actual box of actual dolly mixtures right over with my actual cork!

Trouble is, although I had knocked the dolly mixtures over, I hadn't knocked them OFF the shelf.

Which means the man in the
cowboy hat told me I hadn't won
a prize.

Which wasn't OK. Because now I
was starting to get a bit cross.

CHAPTER 13

The **trouble with getting a bit cross at a funfair** is it makes you need a really big lolly with coloured swirls on it.

Which is lucky really, because guess what I saw when we left the rootin' tootin' shoot 'em stall? Another stall that sold really big lollies with coloured swirls on them!

Nanny said that lollies with coloured swirls on them were better than dolly mixtures any day, and after about six licks I decided she was right.

After about fourteen

licks I decided I was going to try even harder to win a prize at the funfair. Then, about three licks later, I remembered exactly what prize I was going to win first.

A goldfish!!!!!!

The **trouble with going to win a goldfish** is you need to know where to go.

Grampy said he had been keeping an eye out for a stall where I could win a goldfish, but he hadn't seen one anywhere.

I tried looking with two eyes and I couldn't see anywhere either.

Nanny said that when she was my age, just about every stall at the funfair gave you a goldfish in a bag as a prize. Which sounded a bit odd at first, but then Grampy told me the bag was made of plastic and filled with water so the fish could breathe. Which meant that if you won a goldfish in a bag at a funfair, you could take it home and turn it into a pet!

Which made me want to win one even more!

Trouble is, there weren't any

goldfish that I could win.

There were loads of other prizes like teddies with wonky eyes, packs of cards with dragons on, squishy balls, bucket-and-spade sets in springy bags, little plastic guitars and blow-up bananas. But no alive goldfish in filled-up plastic bags.

When Grampy asked a stallholder where all the goldfish were, the stallholder told us that goldfish prizes had been banned from funfairs years

ago. Apparently olden days children used to win goldfish, take them home, but not look after them properly.

Which I can believe actually, because I had a pet goldfish of my own once called Freddy and my mum didn't look after him properly either. She let his water go all green.

Mum said the water was my responsibility, but there was no way that it was. I only said I would look after Freddy. I never EVER said I would look after his water.

In the end Mum gave Freddy to our neighbour, Mrs Pike, to look after, because she had a pond in her garden with nice clean water in it.

Which is a good job really, because if my mum had been left in charge of Freddy, I reckon she would have been arrested by the RSPCA. She might even have gone to prison for goldfish neglect.

The **trouble with Mum going to prison for goldfish neglect** is she wouldn't be able to make my tea.

Or take me to school. Or read me bedtime stories.

So it's probably a good job we couldn't win a goldfish at the funfair.

And anyway, you'll never guess what I suddenly saw next!

Actual POPCORN! I'd never had actual popcorn before!

The **trouble with actual popcorn** is there are two different flavours. Normal and toffee.

The **trouble with normal and toffee** is I like them both the same.

Nanny thought I might have been full after my slush puppy, hotdog, burger, tomato sauce, candyfloss and swirly lolly, but I told her I definitely wasn't.

So she let me have a big box of each!

Trouble is, then I saw the helter-skelter!

The **trouble with helter-skelters** is you're not allowed to go down them with a box of popcorn in each hand.

 I know because when I got to the top of the stairs, the helter-skelter man made me go all the way back down. Which was a bit tricky because there were loads of children coming up the other way.

Nanny and Grampy said they would hold my popcorn for me and meet me at the bottom of the slide. Which was handy really because you need both your hands to go down a helter-skelter slide. One for holding onto your sack, and the other one for waving.

Helter-skelters are one of the highest things you can do at a funfair. When you get to the top of the slide, you can see all the rides and stalls down below you, from one corner of the funfair right over to the other! And you can see all the people who are going bald!

Before you go down the helter-skelter slide, you have to put your legs and bottom inside a sack. Then the helter-skelter man gives you a push, and off you go!

I'd never been on a slide as whizzy as a helter-skelter slide before. Or a slide that was so curly and

bendy! When I got to the bottom I thought I was going to shoot right off the end, but luckily my sack knew when to stop.

Nanny and Grampy asked me if I wanted to go on again, and I nearly did, but then I noticed the hoopla!

The **trouble with the hoopla** is it's
one of the hardest throwing games
in the world.

It looks easy, but when you try it, it actually ends up being really hard.

The way you play hoopla is you give a lady some money, and then she gives you three hoops. Then you have to aim your hoops at some twenty-pound notes that are elastic-banded to some boxes. Real actual twenty-pound notes that you can actually win!

At first I thought you had to throw your hoops over the money to win. But then Nanny told me that my hoop had to go over the money AND the box underneath it as well.

Not just any old over. EXACTLY over.

The **trouble with hoopla hoops** is they have round sides and the boxes have square sides. Which meant my hoops wouldn't fit over the boxes.

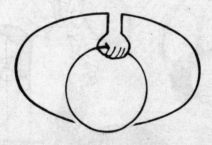

When I asked the hoopla lady for some square hoops, she said she didn't have any. Which meant I couldn't win with my first hoop. I couldn't win with my second hoop.

And I couldn't win with my third hoop either. And neither could Nanny or Grampy.

Which made me feel really, really cross.

Grampy said he'd never won at hoopla in his entire life. Which makes you think, doesn't it? If people can't win at the games, why do the funfair people keep on doing them?

After the hoopla, I was absolutely determined to win a prize. In fact I was so determined and so cross, I decided I wasn't going to go on any other rides AT ALL, UNTIL I HAD WON AN ACTUAL PRIZE ON AN ACTUAL GAME AT THE FUNFAIR!

I wouldn't even go on the octopus until I'd won a prize!

I'm telling you, I was SOOOOO determined . . .

And I was SOOOOOOOOOOOOOOO cross . . .

It made me need an ice cream.

CHAPTER 14

The **trouble with funfair ice creams** is you have to pay more if you want flumps on them.

And you have to pay even more if you want strawberry sauce as well.

Marshmallow flumps are one of my favourite ice-cream sprinkles, and strawberry sauce is one of my

top squirty things in the world. So once
Grampy had given the ice-cream lady
some money, I absolutely
had to have both.

And a flake.

Nanny thought I
must definitely be full

after my slush puppy, hotdog, burger, tomato sauce, candyfloss, swirly lolly and two boxes of popcorn. But the good thing about popcorn is it's really light. So it means you'll always have room for ice cream, flumps, strawberry sauce and a chocolate flake.

Especially on a really hot day.

The **trouble with eating funfair ice creams on really hot days** is you have to eat them really, really quickly.

Otherwise your ice cream will melt, which means your flumps might fall off and your flake might come out. Plus your strawberry sauce might dribble down your cornet and go all over your hand.

Luckily I'm an expert at eating ice creams really, really fast. Which is handy, because if I'd eaten my ice cream any slower, I would absolutely, totally never have been ready to go on . . .

. . . wait for it . . .

Have you guessed it . . . ?

THE COCONUT SHY!!!!!!!

When Grampy told me he'd seen

an actual coconut shy at the funfair, I nearly dropped my last bit of cornet!

A coconut shy isn't a shy coconut, by the way – it's a game where you get to throw really hard balls.

At first I couldn't see the coconut shy anywhere because there were too many people. Luckily Grampy is taller than me so it was easy for him to point the way.

The **trouble with pointing the way** is it still doesn't stop a funfair from being really crowded.

But once we'd squeezed past a really, really long queue for the roller coaster and a much shorter queue for a ride called the teacups, I saw the coconut shy with my very own eyes. Plus I saw the actual coconuts that Grampy said we were going to win! They were sitting on the top of some long sticks that the coconut-shy man had banged into the grass.

At the front, lots of people were lined up, throwing balls at the back of the tent. Every time they hit the back of the tent, the balls dropped down and landed on the grass.

"I can do that! I know I can do that!" I said to Grampy. "All I need is some balls!"

Once Grampy had paid the coconut-shy man some money, I was given five balls of my very own! They were quite small balls, but they were made of hard, roundish wood, which meant they went a really long way when you threw them.

After I'd thrown all five of my balls, I was absolutely sure I'd won a prize, because every single one of my balls hit the back of the tent and every

396

single one of them rolled down and
fell onto the grass!

Just like everybody else's!

Trouble is, that isn't what you have to do to win a coconut. I thought it was, because that's what everyone else was doing.

To win a coconut at a coconut shy, you actually have to knock an actual coconut off an actual stick.

Which means you have to aim at the actual coconuts with your balls.

Grampy said that was what everyone throwing the balls was trying to do. But it didn't look like it to me. Some people weren't even getting close!

Now that I knew the rules of how to play, Nanny said I should have another go. So I did.

Trouble is, I missed all five times again.

The **trouble with missing all five times again** is it makes you start to get cross again.

And it makes you need another go.

Once Nanny had given the man some more money, Grampy stood behind me and told me how to aim. He told me to put one foot forward and one foot back, point at the coconut with my free hand, hold my wooden ball as far back as I could with my throwing hand, close one eye and BLAM IT!

So I did.

But I missed again.

Which made eleven balls I hadn't hit a coconut with. Which made me feel even crosser.

So I aimed again.

The **trouble with aiming at a coconut when you're cross** is it makes your eyes go googly, which means you miss by even more.

Especially if when you let go of the ball, you growl as well.

When Grampy heard me growl, I think he got a bit nervous, so he asked the coconut-shy man if I could stand a bit nearer on my next throw. Which is totally fair because, if you ask me, the more balls you buy, the nearer to the coconuts you should be able to get.

When the coconut-shy man said I could step in front of the line to do my next throw, I was sure I would be able to hit a coconut.

Except I didn't.

I missed again. Or at least my ball did.

Which made me the crossest I'd
been all day. And the growliest.

So Grampy asked if I could stand
a bit nearer still.

The **trouble with standing a bit nearer still** is the coconut-shy man said I was standing too close now. Which I wasn't.

But he said I was. So I had to step back a bit.

Which put me off.

Which meant that I missed with my fourteenth ball as well.

And my fifteenth.

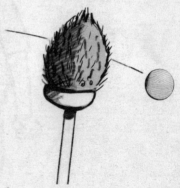

Because I was still feeling a bit put off.

Which made me want to punch all the coconuts and kick all the sticks over. And scream louder than any scream I'd done all day.

But I didn't. Because Grampy said he'd win me a coconut instead.

CHAPTER 15

Once Grampy had paid the coconut-shy man some more money I was sure he'd win me a coconut. But on his first throw he only hit the back of the tent. Grampy said he was just getting his eye in with his first shot, and that he was sure that he would hit a coconut with his second throw.

Trouble is, he didn't. His second ball went

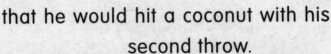

right over the top of the coconuts.

Grampy said that the second ball had slipped out of his hand by mistake and that his third ball had coconut written all over it. (But I don't know who by.)

Then he told us to watch and learn.

The **trouble with watching and learning** is sometimes you're not sure what to watch and learn.

Because not only did Grampy

miss again, he pulled a muscle in his shoulder.

Nanny said it served him right for throwing the ball so hard. Trouble is, now that his shoulder was pulled, Grampy had to retire injured with two balls left to throw!

The **trouble with having two balls left to throw** is you then have to decide who is going to throw them.

I thought I should probably have the last two goes, because I had the most coconut-ball-throwing experience. But then Nanny said, "Why don't we throw one each?"

Which actually was a really good idea, because guess what? You're never going to believe this . . .

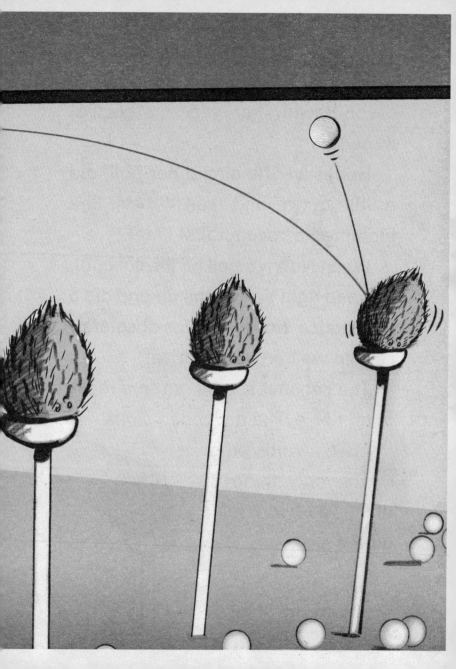

Nanny actually hit an actual coconut with her very first actual throw!!!

Honestly! She aimed her ball, did a little dance and then WHAM! She blammed a coconut first time!

When Nanny's ball hit the coconut, I leaped right up into the air and did a little dance, because I was absolutely certain we had won a prize.

The coconut she hit made a really good noise, like a wooden *clonk*.

Then it wobbled.

The only thing it didn't do was fall off the stick.

Instead of falling off, it just stayed there!

Grampy said Nanny should have thrown her ball harder, but Nanny said if she had, she would have pulled her shoulder too.

I said if you hit a coconut you should win the coconut. Trouble is, the coconut-shy man wouldn't change the rules.

Which made me crosser and more furious than I've ever been in my whole life!

Which is why I threw the last ball at him.

The **trouble with throwing a wooden ball at a coconut-shy man** is if it hits him on the head it could kill him.

Luckily I only hit him on the leg.

Actually, it wasn't even his leg. It was only his knee.

I know it was his knee because it sounded like a coconut.

Nanny and Grampy said they were really disappointed in me

when I threw my last ball at the coconut-shy man. In fact they were so disappointed in me that they made me say sorry.

But guess what? Even though I said sorry, the coconut-shy man STILL banned me from having any more goes. Or from coming within ten metres of his stall.

Which meant now I was NEVER going to win a coconut at the funfair! EVER!

And all because I'd hit a great big coconut-shy man on the leg with a teensy wooden ball!

CHAPTER 16

The **trouble with realizing you're NEVER going to be able to win a coconut EVER in your WHOLE LIFE** is it makes you growl even louder.

Nanny said only grizzly bears were meant to do the kind of growls I was doing and that perhaps it would be better if I sat down on the grass for a

while to calm down.

The **trouble with sitting down on the grass** is it makes me want a toffee apple.

Grampy said there were plenty more prizes we could still win at the fair, but if a toffee apple would stop me growling, it would probably be a good idea.

A toffee apple is an apple dipped in really hard toffee. The toffee is really reddish and you have to bite right through it to get to the juicy apple bit inside.

Nanny said she was amazed I still had room in my tummy for anything, after my slush puppy, hotdog, burger, tomato sauce, candyfloss, swirly lolly, two boxes of popcorn, ice cream, flumps, strawberry sauce and chocolate flake. But toffee apples aren't that filling at all. Because the biggest bit of a toffee apple is made of actual fruit. Plus some of it you can't even eat, like the apple core in the middle or the stick.

Grampy said that once I'd finished nibbling my toffee apple stick we should decide which prize we were going to try and win next. But just as I was putting my toffee apple stick in the bin, we bumped into Mrs Peters!

Mrs Peters said if I kept trying my hardest she was absolutely sure I would win a prize at one of the funfair games soon.

And you'd think she should know, wouldn't you, because she's my teacher.

Trouble is, she was wrong.

The **trouble with the clown bonk** was the clowns kept disappearing before I could bonk them.

The **trouble with the test-your-strength stall** was the hammer was too heavy for me to lift.

The **trouble with hot-shot basketball** was the hoop was too high for me to get the balls in.

The **trouble with tin can alley** was the beanbags I was aiming with went floppy every time I threw them.

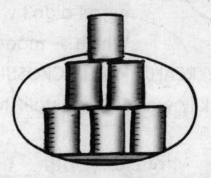

And **the trouble with roll-a-penny** was my pennies wouldn't roll straight at all.

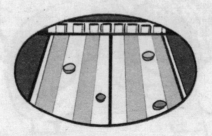

It was hopeless! The harder and harder I tried, the more and more I didn't win!

Which made me REALLY, REALLY, REALLY CROSS!

Luckily we found a stall that sold fudge.

The brilliant thing about fudge is it comes in loads of different square-shaped flavours.

At first I thought I was only allowed one type of flavour fudge in my bag, but the lady in front of us in the queue got three types put in hers.

So I decided to have six flavours: caramel, vanilla, coconut ice, raspberry ripple, chocolate and mint. I was going to have rum and raisin too, but I decided not to in the end, because rum and raisin sounds like it's got beer in it.

Plus I didn't want to be greedy.

Grampy said I should think of

every piece of fudge in my bag as a well-earned prize for trying so hard to win something!

Which made me feel a lot better.

Because when I looked in my bag I still had eight prizes left!

While I was eating a mint one, I thought about ALL the other lovely things that Nanny and Grampy had bought me at the funfair that day – the slush puppy, hotdog, burger, tomato sauce, candyfloss, swirly lolly, two boxes of popcorn, ice cream, flumps, strawberry sauce, chocolate flake and toffee apple. Then I realized that all those were just like prizes too! And I hadn't even had to win them! Nanny and Grampy had just given them to me! That's when I realized what a lucky person I was!

By the time I'd eaten all my squares of fudge, I didn't care about winning actual prizes any more at all! I just decided I was going to have as much fun at the funfair with Nanny and Grampy as I possibly could before it was time to go home.

And boy did we have fun!

First, we went on the big dipper.

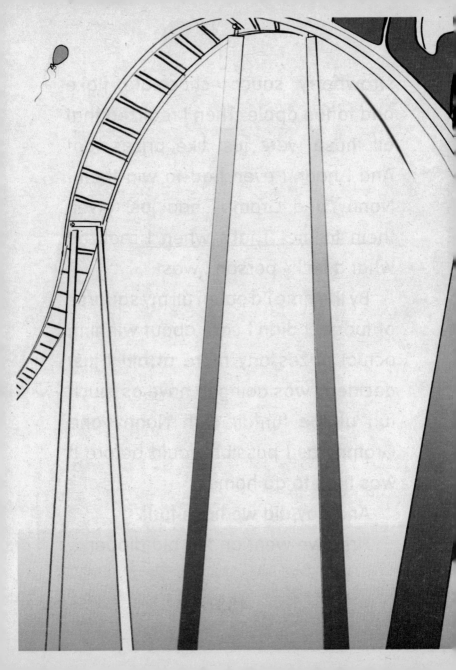

Big dippers are the dippiest things you can do at a funfair.

Then we went on the pirate galleon.

Pirate galleons are the scariest things you can do a funfair. I even saw Dylan doing massive screams!

Then we went in the hall of mirrors!
Halls of mirrors are the funniest-
looking things you can do at a funfair.

Then we went on the octopus! And believe me, Sanjay Lapore was right!

All the rides at the funfair were soooooo much fun! Not just for me, but for all my school friends too!!

I saw Fiona Tucker waving to me on the merry-go-round.

I saw David Alexander pretending to aim at me with the water squirters.

Stephanie Brakespeare got so dizzy on the vortex, she had to go and sit inside an actual St John's ambulance till she felt right again.

Nanny and Grampy said that they wouldn't mind a sit-down too. Not in an ambulance – on a bench.

The **trouble with benches** is they aren't very exciting.

They don't zoom up or down or spin round and round or anything. They ARE free, but after about two seconds, they get really boring.

So Nanny and Grampy said I could go for a little walk by myself. As long as I stayed where they could see me.

That's when I met Jasmine Smart, Nishta Bagwhat, Colin Kettle, Barry Morely, Barry Morely's big brother and two of his friends.

That's when everything started to go a bit wrong.

CHAPTER 17

The **trouble with Jasmine Smart, Nishta Bagwhat, Colin Kettle, Barry Morely, Barry Morely's big brother and two of his friends** is they had all been to the funfair the night before.

And none of them had won on the coconuts either.

Nishta had had ten goes and missed every time.

444

Jasmine had had five goes and got really close.

Colin and Barry had had twenty goes each! Plus Barry had hit the same coconut two times in a row and both times the coconut hadn't fallen off!

When I told them that the same thing had happened to me, Grampy and Nanny, no one was in the slightest bit surprised.

Because do you know what Barry's big brother had told them?

He'd told Barry, Nishta, Jasmine and Colin that the coconuts in the coconut shy at the funfair will never EVER fall off! Because they are stuck on

with super-strength coconut glue!!!!!

And do you know what Barry's big brother's friends had told them as well?

They had told them that the coconuts at the funfair aren't just glued on – there are invisible force fields around all of them too!!

I'd only ever seen invisible force fields in space films before. I never knew you could get them around coconuts. But according to Barry's big brother's friends, the coconut-shy man had a secret force-field gadget in his trouser pocket. Which meant every time he saw you do a good throw he would make you miss by clicking the button and turning a force field on around the coconut you had aimed at!!!

Colin Kettle said that knocking off a glued-on coconut would be a really hard thing to do. And Nishta said knocking off a glued-on coconut with a force field around it would be totally impossible.

Which made me get really cross all over again.

In fact, it made me get so cross, I wanted to scream and growl and stamp my feet all at the same time!!!

Which is why I said I would help Barry, Colin, Nishta and Jasmine tell everyone at the whole funfair what a swizz coconut shies are.

Which is why I said I would join them in a really big coconut-shy protest.

Which is why I said I would meet them at the big wheel at four o'clock.

Which wasn't my fault.

CHAPTER 18

The **trouble with doing a protest** is you're not really sure what a protest is going to be until you've actually done one.

Barry said that his big brother had come up with a really good plan for a protest and that he and his friends were going to give us all the things we needed to make it the best funfair protest ever!

All I had to do was be by the big wheel at four o'clock.

The **trouble with being by the big wheel at four o'clock** is I was meant to be home by four o'clock.

Which meant I had to persuade Nanny and Grampy to stay a little longer. When Nanny looked at her watch and saw it was quarter to four, she said that we really ought to be heading back to the car. But when I told her that the big wheel was the only ride I hadn't had a chance to go on, Grampy persuaded her to stay!

Nanny and Grampy said that they were feeling a bit tired and they would find another bench to sit on and wave to me as I went round. Which was good really, because I wasn't sure if they would want to join in our coconut-shy protest.

When I got to the big wheel, Barry's big brother and his friends were sitting on the grass smiling. Nishta, Jasmine, Colin and Barry were all waiting for me at the end of the queue.

When I joined up with them, we all did a high-five together and then Nishta gave me a big piece of paper to hide under my T-shirt.

Barry told me it was my secret protest poster, but I wasn't allowed to take it out until I got the secret signal.

Then Colin gave me something even more exciting. A tube of superglue!

"We've all got superglue. And we've all got posters," whispered Nishta.

Then they told me the plan.

The **trouble with plans** is they sound really good until they go wrong.

The first bit of our plan went really well, because all we had to do was pay the big-wheel man some money and wait for him to let us on.

The third bit of our plan went really well too.

It was the second bit that got us into trouble.

As soon as the big wheel started to turn, Nishta pulled her poster out from under her T-shirt and held it above her head just like she said she would.

"I'm a coconut!" she shouted at the very top of her voice.

Which was the secret signal for Barry.

"I'm a coconut!" he shouted, holding up his poster too.

461

Which was the secret signal for Jasmine. And then Colin and then me.

By the time all five of us had shouted, "I'm a coconut!" we were right at the top of the big wheel! Which meant everyone in the funfair could see us! And hear us!

Every time the big wheel went back down to the bottom, I waved as hard as I could to Nanny and Grampy. And every time the big wheel went back to the top, I shouted, "I'm a coconut!" as loud as I could to everyone down below!

It was brilliant!

Until the big wheel came to a stop.

The **trouble with big wheels stopping** is everybody expects you to get off. Especially the big-wheel man waiting at the bottom.

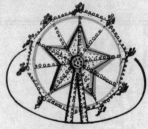

Trouble is, getting off wasn't part of our plan.

Staying on was.

When the big-wheel man asked Nishta to get out of her seat, she shook her head and held her protest poster high up above her head.

Then she began to sing "WE SHALL NOT BE MOVED!"

Which was a signal for us all to start singing too.

When we all started to sing "WE SHALL NOT BE MOVED!" Barry Morely's big brother and his friends started rolling all over the grass and laughing.

The big-wheel man didn't laugh, though. He got cross instead. Mostly I think because he had a long line of people queuing and he couldn't let them on unless we moved.

"Off the wheel NOW!" he said to Nishta. "I've got people waiting to get on!"

That's when Nishta told him that we had glued ourselves to our seats.

The **trouble with telling a big-wheel man that you've glued yourself to your seat** is at first he doesn't believe you.

Especially if it's five seats.

Even nannies and grampies don't believe you.

But when you show them your empty superglue tubes and try to stand up, they change their mind.

Then they call the fire brigade.

The **trouble with calling the fire brigade** is it takes quite a long time for them to arrive.

Which meant I was going to be even later getting home now. Which meant Nanny and Grampy had to call my mum and tell her what I'd done as well.

When the firemen arrived at the funfair and found out that we were coconuts glued to our seats, they told Nanny that they were going to

have to cut a hole in my new orange shorts.

And my pants.

Which was a bit embarrassing really. Especially for Colin, because he didn't have any pants on.

It took the firemen about two hours to cut Nishta, Barry, Jasmine, Colin and me out of our seats. And after that, the big wheel had to be closed for repairs. Which made the big-wheel man go the same colour as my slush puppy.

When he threatened to sue Nishta's mum and dad for loss of earnings, Nanny and Grampy went a

bit of a funny colour too. Then they
suggested we walk back to the car
as quickly as we could.

On the way, Grampy told me

that we had been tricked into doing something very silly by Barry Morely's big brother and his big-boy friends. That's why they were rolling all over the grass and laughing at us so much as we went round and round on the big wheel.

Which made me start growling all over again.

Nanny said that big boys can be really immature sometimes and that from now on it might be better if me and my friends ignored anything we ever heard big boys say. Especially big-boy talk about coconuts, glue and invisible force fields.

When we got near to the coconut shy, I realized that Nanny and Grampy were right.

Because just as we walked past, I saw an actual coconut being knocked off an actual stick by an actual wooden ball.

When the boy who had thrown the ball turned round, put his shirt over his head and started running around like a footballer who had scored a goal, I nearly screamed!

Because do you know who it was?!

Do you know who had won an actual coconut at the funfair, with one really good throw?

It was JACK BEECHWHISTLE!

Of all the boys in all the funfair, it had to be HIM!

I was growling like a grizzly bear crossed with a dinosaur by the time I got back to the car.

CHAPTER 19

I didn't get home till twenty to seven this evening. Which isn't my bedtime, but for some unknown reason Mum has decided it is.

Nanny and Grampy said they were pleased that I'd had such a lovely time, but it might be a while before they took me to a funfair again.

Mum said that gluing myself to a piece of funfair equipment was an extremely silly thing to do and that ruining my new orange shorts was disgraceful. She said the hole in my

shorts was so big, she would have to throw them away. Which if you ask me, means she is just too lazy to sew them up.

Anyway, as a punishment, she said I would be going to bed without any grilled chicken, wild rice and broccoli for supper.

Which is OK
actually. Because, to
be honest, I am
still a bit full
from my slush
puppy, hotdog,
burger, tomato sauce,
candyfloss, swirly
lolly, two boxes
of popcorn, ice
cream, flumps,
strawberry sauce,

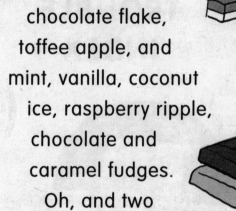

chocolate flake,
toffee apple, and
mint, vanilla, coconut
ice, raspberry ripple,
chocolate and
caramel fudges.
Oh, and two
of Nanny's mints. (I had
another one on the way
home!)

Tee-hee!

P.S. I bet you thought
I was going to be sick!

DAISY'S
TROUBLE
INDEX

The trouble with . . .

Daisy's Kittens Quiz!

1. What is the Spanish word
    for kittens?

2. What three things did Daisy's
    mum buy her before her
    birthday?

3. What did Daisy leave in the
    airport lounge?

4. How high up was the plane
    that Daisy travelled on?

5.   What did Daisy name the kittens?

6.   What is Dylan's snake called?

7.   What did Daisy name her imaginary black bull and donkey?

8.   Why did Daisy and Harrison get told off by the hotel manager?

9.   How old is Harrison?

10.   What did Daisy spend her holiday money on?

The answers are at the back of the book!

Daisy's Coconuts Quiz!

1. Who was the third person to tell Daisy about the funfair coming to town?

2. What did David Alexander draw on his backpack?

3. Grampy tells Daisy that they absolutely must win two things at the funfair – what are they?

4. What two types of cereal does Daisy use to make her special funfair breakfast?

5. Daisy got the numbers 3, 6 and 9 in the tombola - why didn't she win a prize with these numbers?

6. What was the number on the side of Daisy's bumper car?

7. Daisy asks for a red slush puppy mixed with bright blue – what colour does this make?

8. On what part of the body does Daisy hit the coconut shy man with the ball?

9. What three words do Daisy and her friends shout at the top of the big wheel?

10. Why did the fire brigade have to cut a hole in Daisy's new shorts?

The answers are at the back of the book!

Test your memory!

To play this fun holiday game you need at least one friend with you.

One person says, 'When I went on holiday, I packed my suitcase and in it I put . . .' followed by any object – for example, 'a swimming costume.'

The next person then says, 'I packed my suitcase and in it I put a swimming costume,' and then adds their own item – for example, 'a pair of flip flops.'

This keeps on going until any of the people playing forget any of the items, or can't think of a new item to add!

Daisy's Funfair Wordsearch

Can you find these words in the wordsearch below?

funfair	dodgems	protest
coconuts	forcefield	candyfloss
suncream	superglue	waltzer
tombola		popcorn

i	x	x	w	f	o	w	o	k	h	e	h	a
a	c	p	o	p	c	o	r	n	s	k	u	f
t	a	y	y	e	s	d	r	m	u	c	o	o
k	n	t	a	g	c	a	e	t	p	o	h	r
p	d	o	n	f	w	g	a	f	e	c	n	c
l	y	m	b	m	d	q	r	t	r	o	w	e
y	f	b	c	o	f	i	j	l	g	n	a	f
c	l	o	d	u	a	f	g	a	l	u	l	i
b	o	l	f	f	l	w	m	c	u	t	z	e
w	s	a	n	n	p	r	o	t	e	s	t	l
d	s	u	n	c	r	e	a	m	a	z	r	d
a	f	w	d	w	a	l	t	z	e	r	e	i

Daisy's Secret Code!

Daisy has sent you a secret message from her holiday! Use this secret code to find out what it is:

A	B	C	D	E	F	G	H	I	J	K	L	M
1	2	3	4	5	6	7	8	9	10	11	12	13

N	O	P	Q	R	S	T	U	V	W	X	Y	Z
14	15	16	17	18	19	20	21	22	23	24	25	26

19 8 8,   9'13   20 1 11 9 14 7   1

11 9 20 20 5 14   8 15 13 5   23 9 20 8   13 5!

Spot the difference!

Can you spot the ten differences between these pictures?

Daisy's Tasty Toffee Apples

Daisy enjoys toffee apples so much that she wants to share some with you! Here is a recipe for some delicious toffee apples. (Make sure you ask an adult to help you!)

You will need:

4 apples

200g caster sugar

4 tablespoons golden syrup

A drop of vinegar

Decoration, e.g. sprinkles or marshmallows (optional)

Method:

1. Put the apples in a big bowl with some warm water, and give them a wash.

2. Dry them off with a tea towel and pull out all the stalks.

3. Put the sugar in a pan with around 50ml water and stir it until all the sugar has dissolved. Then gradually add the syrup and vinegar and keep stirring.

4. When the toffee begins to thicken, take it off the heat, then dunk the apples in. Make sure they are fully covered in the toffee mixture!

5. Put the apples on a tray and leave them to cool for a few hours.

6. Once the toffee has set, add some decoration, if you want to, like sprinkles or marshmallows!

Test Your Memory!

Can you remember all the things
Daisy ate at the funfair?
Try not to look back at the story!

_____

_____

_____

_____

_____

_____

_____

_____

_____

_____

_____

_____

Match the Spanish

Daisy learns some Spanish on her holiday!

Can you match up these English words with the Spanish words?

Kittens	Playa
Friend	Problema
Holiday	Amigo
Beach	Vacaciones
Plane	Gatito
Trouble	Avión

Daisy's Holiday Wordsearch

Can you find these words in the wordsearch below?

swim   aeroplane   fleas
kittens   octopus   sun
beetle   beach   holiday
rucksack

s	r	t	n	f	l	e	a	s	b	a	s	s
u	s	h	n	n	u	t	w	f	a	b	u	n
a	r	w	t	b	s	h	n	k	e	n	l	t
h	o	l	i	d	a	y	e	y	r	a	s	d
a	f	d	n	m	q	s	k	c	o	g	f	k
b	e	a	c	h	u	i	c	u	p	q	z	i
d	a	n	z	p	u	t	a	a	l	a	n	t
o	m	s	o	l	p	t	s	h	a	n	d	t
r	t	t	h	n	f	s	k	a	n	l	v	e
p	c	i	l	m	t	r	c	h	e	b	q	n
o	s	p	a	y	d	e	u	r	h	r	s	s
b	e	e	t	l	e	t	r	o	c	t	b	h

Design your own Funfair Ride

The Big Wheel is out of service, so the funfair needs to find a replacement! Can you design a replacement ride for the funfair?

Write your holiday checklist!

Imagine you're going on holiday
to Spain, like Daisy.
What would you pack in your suitcase?
Daisy has started you off:

- [x] Sun cream
- [x] Swimming costume
- [ ]
- [ ]
- [ ]
- [ ]
- [ ]
- [ ]
- [ ]
- [ ]
- [ ]
- [ ]
- [ ]

Make your own delicious strawberry milk lollies!

These are perfect for a hot summery day.
Make sure you ask a grown-up for help!

You will need:
400g ripe strawberries
200ml semi-skimmed milk
400g can condensed milk
10-12 ice-lolly moulds

What to do:

1. Carefully cut the green leafy bit from the strawberries, and then chop each strawberry in half.

2. Put the strawberries in a food processor and blend up until you have a smooth paste.

3. Add the milk and condensed milk and blend again until creamy.

4. Carefully pour the mixture into your ice-lolly moulds and pop into the freezer for up to four hours until frozen solid.

5. Enjoy!

Have you read these other Daisy books?

Have you read these other Daisy books?

Answers

Daisy's Coconuts Quiz:

1. Daniel McNicholl
2. A rifle range with exploding ducks
3. A coconut, a goldfish
4. Weetabix and Honey Nut Loops
5. Because they don't end in a zero
6. 8
7. Light Purple
8. Knee
9. I'm a coconut
10. Because she had superglued herself to the seat

Daisy's Kittens Quiz:

1. Gatitos
2. Swimming costume, flip-flops, sun cream
3. Her rucksack
4. 37,000 feet
5. Miffy, Marble, Midnight, Mini Moo and Smoky
6. Shooter
7. Blackie and Giddyup
8. They stole a whole salmon
9. Eight years old
10. Cat food!

Daisy's Secret Code!

Shh, I'm taking a kitten home with me!

Daisy's Funfair Wordsearch:

i	x	x	w	f	o	w	o	k	h	e	h	a
a	c	p	o	p	c	o	r	n	s	k	u	f
t	a	y	y	e	s	d	r	m	u	c	o	o
k	n	t	a	g	c	a	e	t	p	o	h	r
p	d	o	n	f	w	g	a	f	e	c	n	c
l	y	m	b	m	d	q	r	t	r	o	w	e
y	f	b	c	o	f	i	j	l	g	n	a	f
c	l	o	d	u	a	f	g	a	l	u	l	i
b	o	l	f	l	w	m	c	u	t	z	e
w	s	a	n	n	p	r	o	t	e	s	t	l
d	s	u	n	c	r	e	a	m	a	z	r	d
a	f	w	d	w	a	l	t	z	e	r	e	i

Match the Spanish

Kittens	Gatito
Friend	Amigo
Holiday	Vacaciones
Beach	Playa
Plane	Avión
Trouble	Problema

Spot the difference!

Daisy's Holiday Wordsearch:

s	r	t	n	f	l	e	a	s	b	a	s	s
u	s	h	n	n	u	t	w	f	a	b	u	n
a	r	w	t	b	s	h	n	k	e	n	l	t
h	o	l	i	d	a	y	e	y	r	a	s	d
a	f	d	n	m	q	s	k	c	o	g	f	k
b	e	a	c	h	u	i	c	u	p	q	z	i
d	a	n	z	p	u	t	a	a	l	a	n	t
o	m	s	o	l	p	t	s	h	a	n	d	t
r	t	t	h	n	f	s	k	a	n	l	v	e
p	c	i	l	m	t	r	c	h	e	b	q	n
o	s	p	a	y	d	e	u	r	h	r	s	s
b	e	e	t	l	e	t	r	o	c	t	b	h